From the "Pe... Column of the *EASTWICK GAZETTE*

Apparently one of the blond, blue-blooded organizers of the Autumn Ball had a wee bit too much bubbly. Sources say this Eastwick socialite and her husband had a very public tiff before he escorted her home.

Privately, some have speculated that this couple's marriage is on the rocks despite some hot-and-heavy reconciliations. After all, the husband in question is away on business *a lot*, causing some to whisper about another woman. And there are rumors about divorce papers being served.

But if that's the case, why are they still living under the same fabulous roof? Are they sharing the same bed or sleeping solo? Unfortunately, attempts to learn more have met with resistance—who knew asking a few simple questions would be like trying to break in to Fort Knox?

We'll keep you posted about all developments— the good, the bad...and the baby. (Just another little rumor...)

Dear Reader,

What if you found out the man you married wasn't who he said he was at all? Would you be able to forgive him for lying to you—if he had a really good reason?

In *The Part-Time Wife,* Abby Baldwin is finding out all sorts of interesting things about her husband, Luke Talbot. And Luke is caught between the lies he's told and the woman he loves more than anything.

I had so much fun being a part of the SECRET LIVES OF SOCIETY WIVES continuity. I hope you enjoy your time in Eastwick as much as all the authors did! And I hope you'll continue to buy and read Silhouette Desire novels— we love writing them for you.

Love,

Maureen

P.S. Be sure to check out my Web site, www.maureenchild.com, for information about my newest releases, including my first Silhouette Nocturne novel, *Eternally,* on sale this November wherever Silhouette Books are sold.

MAUREEN CHILD

THE PART-TIME WIFE

Published by Silhouette Books
America's Publisher of Contemporary Romance

Special thanks and acknowledgment are given
to Maureen Child for her contribution to the
SECRET LIVES OF SOCIETY WIVES miniseries.

 SILHOUETTE BOOKS
®

ISBN-13: 978-0-373-76755-7
ISBN-10:   0-373-76755-2

THE PART-TIME WIFE

Visit Silhouette Books at www.eHarlequin.com

Printed in U.S.A.

Recent Books by Maureen Child

Silhouette Desire

Man Beneath the Uniform #1561
Lost in Sensation #1611
Society-Page Seduction #1639
*The Tempting Mrs. Reilly #1652
*Whatever Reilly Wants #1658
*The Last Reilly Standing #1664
**Expecting Lonergan's Baby #1719
**Strictly Lonergan's Business #1724
**Satisfying Lonergan's Honor #1730
The Part-Time Wife #1755

Summer in Savannah
"With a Twist"

Silhouette Special Edition

Forever...Again #1604

*Three-Way Wager
** Summer of Secrets

MAUREEN CHILD

is a California native who loves to travel. Every chance they get, she and her husband are taking off on another research trip. The author of more than sixty books, Maureen loves a happy ending and still swears that she has the best job in the world. She lives in Southern California with her husband, two children and a golden retriever with delusions of grandeur.

For my niece, Maegan Carberry, because she always wanted a dedication all to herself! Love you, Mae!

One

"Let's hear it for the Debs!" Abby Baldwin Talbot said, lifting her champagne glass in a toast to the five women who were her best friends.

"Way to go, us!" Felicity chimed in and the others lifted their glasses, as well.

Abby looked from one to the other of them and smiled at each in turn. There were the original members of the Debs Club…girls who'd gone through Eastwick Academy together and survived their "coming-out" society debut arm in arm. Emma, Mary, Felicity and Abby had known each other forever and their bond was unbreakable. But if it couldn't break, it did bend, at least far enough to welcome two new members into their circle. Lily and Vanessa had slipped into the group seamlessly and now Abby couldn't imagine her life without all of these women in it.

Especially now, she thought, but didn't say. With everything else in her world crumbling around her, she needed the familiarity, the love she found with her friends more than ever.

"Okay, hate to break up the moment," Mary said with a quick grin. "But as much as I love you guys, I want to claim a dance with Kane." Then her grin faded a little as she asked, "You all right, Abby?"

"I'm terrific," she lied, smile wide. She took another sip of champagne to ease the dryness in her throat. "Go. Boogie the night away."

"Sounds like a plan," Felicity agreed.

"Right behind you," Vanessa said, then glanced at the three remaining women standing at the back of the country club ballroom. "You guys coming?"

"I am," Lily said, smoothing the front of her gown unnecessarily.

"I'll be along in a few minutes," Abby told her friends. "I just want to stand back here and watch the party for a while."

"Okay," Vanessa told her, pointing her index finger at her. "But if you're not out on the dance floor in fifteen minutes, I'm coming to find you."

Abby nodded. "Consider me warned."

Vanessa and Lily dissolved into the crowd and Abby took a long, deep breath. It was agonizing trying to keep up a cheerful front for the people she loved best. But damned if she would ruin this party they'd all worked so hard on. With that thought firmly in mind, she glanced up at her much taller friend.

"You did an amazing job on this place, Emma."

"You mean *we* did an amazing job," Emma countered, as her gaze drifted around the crowded, noisy ballroom.

It seemed as though everyone in Eastwick had turned out for this year's Autumn Ball. Diamonds winked at throats and ears, and hands glittered with enough jewelry to give a security company a collective heart attack. Women wore bright colored gowns as if trying to enliven the fall and stave off the coming winter. They greeted each other with hugs and air kisses, then whispered with their friends about everyone else in the room. Men in tuxedos gathered in tight knots to talk about whatever it was men found so fascinating. Football? The stock market?

Didn't matter, Abby told herself. All that mattered was, that the Debs Club had managed to make the old country club shine for the night. Soft lights, a live band playing old standards with a few classic rock-and-roll songs tossed in for flavor. A champagne fountain—tacky, but fun—stood proudly in the middle of the room and sharply dressed waiters moved through the crowds, balancing trays of artfully arranged canapés.

The Debs Club.

Abby smiled and thought about that. She and her friends had nicknamed themselves the Debs in honor of the night they'd been society debutantes. It had all seemed so silly, so old-fashioned back then. But the friendships forged in high school and at that cotillion had stood the test of time. Now here they were, years later, still a force to be reckoned with.

So much had changed, though, Abby thought, glancing around the room and picking out the faces of her friends. So many things had happened over the past several months, that she could sense a strained atmosphere in the room, as if everyone present were holding their breath, waiting for the next bombshell to hit.

And who could blame them? Murder and extortion were just not the norm in Eastwick. Or at least, they never used to be.

Abby's eyes filled with tears and she wasn't sure if her blurry vision was from the attempt not to cry or the champagne she'd been drinking steadily since she arrived. She probably should have had something to eat, but she simply hadn't been able to even consider choking down food. Not with her stomach in knots and her nerves jangling.

This was all Luke's fault, she told herself grimly, as her husband's face rose up in her mind. He should have been here. Had *promised* to be here. But, like most of Luke Talbot's promises, they weren't worth the breath he used to make them.

"Ab?" Emma asked, staring into her eyes, "Are you okay?"

Oh, she hadn't been okay for a long time. And she

was getting less okay with every passing day. *Less okay?* That sounded stupid. She met Emma's violet gaze and did what she'd been doing for months now. She lied to one of her best friends.

"I'm *fine,* Emma." She plastered her practiced smile on her face and inhaled sharply. "Really. I'm good. Better than good," she said and stepped closer, stumbling just a bit on the hem of her cranberry-colored, floor-length gown.

"Hey, careful," Emma urged.

"Oh, I'm always careful," Abby said. "That's me. Careful Abby. Always looking before she leaps. Always doing the right thing. Always— What were we talking about?"

Emma frowned at her, then shifted a look around the room, as if searching for backup. Giving up, she said, "I think you should come and sit down for a while. I'll get you something to eat."

"Not hungry. I'm just enjoying myself, Em. No worries." Abby took another sip of her champagne, slipped her arm through the crook of Emma's and whispered, "We all worked really hard to pull this ball off— you more than anyone. So let's just party tonight."

"I think you've had enough party."

"Emma." Waving with her champagne glass, Abby said "Oops," as some of the bubbling wine sloshed over the crystal rim to drip down the back of her hand. "I'm fine, fine," she insisted as Emma stopped a passing waiter to snag a couple of cocktail napkins. "Everything's good."

"Abby, how much of that champagne have you had?"

"Not nearly enough," Abby answered, the fake smile she'd been wearing all night slipping just a little.

Her world was crashing down around her and nobody knew it but she and the man she'd once thought she knew so well. What would the Debs have to say if they knew she'd seen a lawyer? If they knew that she was having Luke served with divorce papers? If they knew what Abby had only discovered the week before—that she'd married a liar, a cheat, a *bastard*.

She took another gulp of air, straightened and blinked the blurries out of her vision. Facing Emma, she lifted her chin and said, "I'm really fine, Em. Go find that new husband of yours and have some fun, okay? I'm just going to go sit down on the patio."

"It's freezing out there," Emma countered.

"I have a wrap. I'll be fine." To prove it, Abby tossed her black cashmere stole across her left shoulder, then set her nearly empty glass of champagne down on a passing waiter's tray. "See? I'm good. Go. Play. Dance."

"Okay…" Emma bent down to plant a kiss on Abby's cheek. "But I'll catch up with you again later."

"I'll be here," Abby quipped, making her smile brighter, her voice lighter. *Alone,* she added silently.

She watched as Emma moved through the crowd, stopping to say hello, smiling at friends, then finally, being swooped into her new husband Garrett's welcoming embrace. As the two deliriously happy people began to dance, an awful sense of envy crawled through Abby.

God, she was a terrible human being. How could she begrudge Emma her hard-won happiness? Answer? Abby didn't. Not really. But oh, how she wanted to feel that way again. She could remember so clearly how she'd felt when she and Luke had first gotten together. She remembered that quickening of her pulse, the jumping in the pit of her stomach.

But it had been so long since she'd felt anything but *alone*, she wanted to weep for the loss of what she and her husband had once had.

Now, she was standing in a crowded ballroom, surrounded by people and she felt lonelier than she could ever remember feeling. The music washed over her. A soft, cool breeze drifted in through the open French doors leading onto the patio. Laughter, snatches of conversation rose in the air and settled over her like an uncomfortable blanket.

"Shouldn't have come," she whispered, low enough that no one around her could overhear.

Of course, she'd had to show up. The Debs were responsible for the success of the ball and she had owed it to her friends to be here. But God, she wished she were anywhere else. She could hardly stand being at the club anymore. Nothing was the same. Nothing felt…safe anymore.

A chill that had nothing to do with the late-October air swept along her spine. Staring at the faces in the crowd, she didn't see familiarity. She saw suspicion. She saw guilt. Fear. Ever since discovering that the death of her mother, Bunny Baldwin, hadn't been an accident, but murder, Abby had been forced to admit that perhaps everyone she knew and trusted weren't what they seemed.

Starting with her husband.

And God help her, in spite of everything, she wished that he were there with her right now. Not as he was now, though. But as he had been when they'd first met. First fell in love. Wistfully, she blanked out the ball she cared nothing about and let memories swarm through her mind.

The day after her graduation from college, Abby struck out on her first adventure. Two weeks in Paris. Alone. She had plans to explore the city, sit at sidewalk cafés and look properly bored. She wanted to drink wine in a park, see the Eiffel Tower and wander through Notre Dame.

She had planned every minute of the trip she'd been looking forward to for years. There wasn't a single impulsive bone in her body. She believed in organization. Clarity. Plans. She even had an itinerary, which went right out the window the minute Luke Talbot took the seat beside her on the flight to France.

She watched him enter the plane and look around and she held her breath until he came to her row of seats and smiled down at her.

"Well, this long flight suddenly looks a lot more

interesting," he said, and stowed his carry-on above the first-class seats. Then he dropped into the aisle seat beside hers and held out his right hand. "Luke Talbot."

As soon as she touched him, Abby knew this moment was…special. Different. Something hot and exciting and totally unexpected zinged from her palm up the length of her arm and then rattled around in her chest like a BB in the bottom of an empty can.

She looked into his eyes and couldn't look away. "Abby Baldwin."

He released her hand reluctantly and Abby folded her fingers into her palm as if trying to hold on to that jolt of electrical energy.

"First trip to Paris?" he asked.

"How can you tell?" Abby wondered.

"There's excitement in your eyes."

"Really?" she asked, just a little disappointed. "And here I was trying to look like an experienced world traveler."

"Oh, this is better. Trust me."

Abby's stomach dipped and rolled as his dark brown eyes collided with hers. His hair, also dark brown, was shaggy, a little rumpled and he wore a gray sweater with blue jeans. He looked a little collegiate and very sexy. What better way to start her adventure than with a little flirting?

"What about you?" she asked. "First time to Paris?"

His eyes darkened a bit, then the shadows lifted again and he shook his head. "Nope. I make this trip pretty regularly for business."

"What do you do?"

"I'm a rep for a software company." He gave her a slow smile. "What about you?"

"I just graduated from college."

"Congratulations—a degree in what?"

"Thanks—and my degree's in communications. Minor in foreign languages."

"Well, that's disappointing," he said, his gaze moving over her features. "I was sort of hoping you'd need an interpreter."

She smiled, enjoying the twist and pull of nerves in the pit of her stomach. "I don't need an interpreter," she admitted then took a breath and a risk at the same time. She couldn't believe she was going to do this. She didn't even know this guy. But something inside her demanded that she *get* to know him. "But if you're interested, I could use a guide who knows his way around Paris."

His mouth curved in a smile that sent a lightning-like bolt of sheer lust slicing through her.

"I'd like that, Abby Baldwin."

She jolted a little and grabbed hold of the armrest as the plane lurched into the taxi down the runway.

"Nervous about flying?" he asked, covering her hand with his own.

"A little," she admitted, through gritted teeth. "Well, not the actual flying part. That's okay. It's the takeoff that gets me. I never really believe they're going to be able to get up into the air."

He picked her hand up off the armrest, cradled it between both of his and said, "Believe, Abby. The plane will go up and we'll discover Paris together."

And they had, she thought on a sigh. For two weeks, they'd spent nearly every moment with each other. Sure, Luke had had to work, but mostly, it had been just the two of them.

Sweet little bistros, dancing in the dark to the music from a street musician just beneath the Eiffel Tower, its light glittering in the darkness. Shared wine and fresh baguettes, picnics along the banks of the Seine and long, slow afternoons, locked away in a tiny hotel room three stories above a loud, bustling alley.

They'd made love for hours, discovering each other over and over again. Their bodies were joined, their hearts engaged and before the two weeks were over, they each knew that their lives would never be the same again.

Tugging her cashmere wrap tighter around her shoulders, Abby sighed and headed for the French doors leading to the balcony. Luke had proposed on that last, wonderful night in Paris. He'd kissed her in front of the Louvre, and promised to love her forever.

She'd been so blinded by happiness, so lost in

love, she had never questioned what they felt for each other. When he'd reminded her that he would have to travel for business, she hadn't cared. Knowing that he would be coming home to her was more than enough.

Love caught them both unawares.

And now, so many years later, it wasn't love keeping them together. Now it was just habit. A habit, Abby told herself, that it was more than time to break.

"Champagne, ma'am?" A waiter asked, pausing beside her and giving her a half bow.

She looked past him to the man hurrying across the crowded room to her side. Luke. He had finally arrived after all.

And she wished desperately that her heart hadn't leaped into her throat with just one look at him. How could she still love him, even knowing that he'd been lying to her for who knew how many years?

"Ma'am?" the waiter prodded gently. "Champagne?"

"Yes," she said, reaching for the glass. "I think I will."

Two

Luke Talbot slipped through the crowd, hardly causing a ripple of awareness from the people around him. But even if he had, he wouldn't have cared—or noticed. His gaze was locked on his wife.

He was late, but there'd been no way to avoid it. Hell, it was a miracle he'd been able to make it to the ball at all. But he knew how hard Abby and her friends had worked to make this event a success and he'd wanted to be here. For her.

Not entirely true, he thought as he got closer to the wife who didn't look particularly happy to see him. He'd wanted to be here because being away from Abby was miserable.

He was the first to admit that his trips for work

were necessary. He knew that his job was an important one and he consoled himself with the fact that he had warned Abby going into this marriage that he would have to be gone. A lot. But it was getting harder and harder to leave her.

When he was close enough to look directly into her pale blue eyes, he clearly saw the gleam of emotion stirring there. She was furious. Maybe no one else would see it. But Luke did.

"Babe," he said, forcing a smile to combat the light of battle in her eyes, "I made it."

"So I see."

He leaned in to kiss her and she stepped back hastily, stumbling slightly before she could catch her balance. His eyes narrowed on the still-full glass of champagne she clutched in a white-knuckle grip. "How much of that stuff have you had?"

"That really isn't any of your business, is it?" she asked through gritted teeth.

God, even furious, Abby was enough to take his breath away. That soft blond hair of hers was pulled up at the back of her head and the blond ends sprayed out into a fall of gold. She wore the ruby necklace he'd given her on their first Christmas together and the thumb-sized stone lay nestled in her cleavage, displayed proudly by the dark red gown she was wearing. The matching earrings, an anniversary present, shone darkly at her ears like drops of blood against her pale, white skin and he cringed inwardly at the metaphor.

She wasn't tall, but every inch of her was packed nicely. She was the kind of woman who haunted a man's dreams. His, anyway. And she had from the first moment he'd met her.

"Why are you here, Luke?" she asked, her voice a touch louder now.

"What's that supposed to mean?" he countered, glancing around him to make sure no one was listening.

"It means," she said tightly, "I can't quite figure out why you would even bother to show up at the ball."

"I told you I'd be here."

"Oh." She nodded and her mouth twisted into a parody of a smile. "And you never lie to me, do you, Luke?"

Slippery ground here, he thought and stuffed his hands into his pockets to keep from grabbing her. The safest answer was the one he usually took. Answer a question with a question. Distract and disarm. "Why would I lie to you, babe?"

"Just what I was wondering," she said, her voice lifting a notch or two. Enough to have a couple of the people closest to them turning to glance their way.

"Abby…" He glared at the older man beside him and the guy turned away, but Luke wasn't stupid enough to believe he'd stopped listening. "This isn't the place to—"

"To what?" she asked, swinging her champagne glass wide and sloshing some of its contents onto the floor. "To talk about why my *husband* lies to me?"

Luke gritted his teeth, pulled his hands from his pockets and made a grab for her. She stepped back quickly, though, and the way she was avoiding his touch cut at him.

"I didn't lie to you." *Until right this minute,* he thought with an inward groan.

He had been so damn careful over the years. Always couching his excuses in half-truths. Disguising everything he said in shades of gray, so that he could reassure himself in the middle of lonely nights that he wasn't actually *lying* to the woman he loved.

Should have known that couldn't last forever.

"Liar," she whispered and her voice carried the sting of hurt. Louder, she said, "I called you at your hotel in Sacramento a couple of days ago."

Confused, he said, "Yeah. I know. We talked for like a half an hour."

"Hah!" She lifted her chin and looked down at him. Not easy considering she was nearly six inches shorter than Luke. "But I called the hotel before that, too," she said and started swaying unsteadily.

Luke's gaze narrowed on the champagne. Clearly she'd already had too much. "Abby…"

"I didn't have the number you gave me in my purse, so I called information and got the hotel's phone number myself."

Oh, God.

"Wanna know what they said?" she taunted, and her voice lifted again. Loud enough now that several people were turning to listen.

"I think you've had all the champagne you need," he said and snatched her glass from her hand.

"Hey! I wasn't finished with that."

"Oh yeah, you were," he said, clutching the glass with one hand and catching her elbow with the other. Determinedly, he turned her around, steered her through the French doors and out onto the semideserted stone patio.

Out here, the music was softer. Conversations were no more than a rippling undercurrent of sound. The couples besides Luke and Abby who had braved the chilly October night air, were sprinkled around the large patio, giving them a semblance of privacy.

He had a feeling they were going to need it. Setting the flute down on the patio railing, he let go of Abby when she yanked herself free.

Below them, the manicured golf course stretched out in shadowy acres lit by the moon and a few discreetly placed lawn lamps. Pools of light formed on the grass and splintered against the trees that lined the fairway. In the adjacent parking lot, a car's engine growled into life and water danced eagerly in a fountain at the far edge of the patio.

Abby looked at him and Luke wanted nothing more than to pull her into his arms—but he knew she wouldn't welcome it. Her eyes were filled with hurt and it tore at him to see her features twisted with pain *he* had caused. He hadn't meant to hurt her. Ever. But he'd known all along that it would happen eventually.

"The hotel in Sacramento never *heard* of you,

Luke," she said, swinging her cashmere wrap around her shoulders and holding on to it tightly. A single strand of blond hair fell across her eyes and she whipped her head back to toss it aside. "You weren't registered there. Had *never* been registered there."

Damn it.

A shaky laugh escaped her throat. "I explained how you always stayed there when you were in town. That I'd spoken to you in your room only two days before." Her blue eyes narrowed on him. "They thought I was crazy."

"I can explain…" Not really. But he'd try. God help him, he'd try.

She held up one hand for silence. "When I got home, I used the number *you* left with me and voilà! The hotel operator—a woman with a very deep, very sexy voice, by the way—put me right through to your 'room.' Interesting, isn't it?"

"Abby, there's a perfectly reasonable explanation." She'd never believe the truth, so he'd have to find an alternate story to tell. Fast.

"Of course there is!" She kept one hand on her wrap and reached up with the other to push that loose strand of hair irritating her back into place. "It's all very clear to me now," she said, her words beginning to slur just a little.

He reached out to steady her when she stumbled again and she leaped back.

"Don't touch me again," she muttered thickly. "I don't want you to touch me."

He winced as though her words had actually delivered a physical blow.

"You lied to me, Luke," she said and for the first time, he saw tears pool in her eyes. "Maybe you've been lying to me all along. Is that it? Right from the beginning?"

"No, Abby," he said hotly, half expecting his tongue to fall off with yet another lie. "No."

She shook her head, unconvinced. "A couple of months ago, Delia Forrester hinted that when you left me, you weren't really off on business trips. That you were with other women."

Delia Forrester. A woman with a sharp mind and a calculator for a heart. At forty, her husband, Frank, was thirty years older than she and, though she seemed to dote on the man, she didn't have too much trouble coming on to younger guys. Including Luke. He'd brushed her off as politely as possible, but now, it looked as though she'd found a way to get back at him for refusing her.

"Delia Forrester's a bitch and you know it."

"Doesn't mean she was wrong," Abby countered quickly. "I stood up for you, you know. Defended my *husband*. Now I have to wonder. Are you really my husband? Are we even legally married?"

"Of course we are. Hell, we got married right here," he reminded her in a tight, hot voice. "In this club."

"Doesn't make it legal," she said, slowly shaking her head. "Doesn't mean you don't have twenty other wives all over the damn country. Heck." She hiccuped, covered her mouth and whispered, "Maybe even a few in Europe."

"What?" he demanded. "Now I'm a bigamist?"

"Why not?" she argued. "You lie to me so well, that tells me you get plenty of practice." She stepped in close, put both hands on his chest and gave him a hard shove that didn't budge him. Her wrap fell down to her elbows and she snatched it back up. "Our whole life is a *lie,* Luke. I can't believe anything you've ever said to me. For all I know, you met me on that plane on purpose. To set me up. To marry me and pretend to love me and then to—"

Luke's heart twisted as she ranted, but he knew he'd never slow her down now, so he let her go on. Get it all out. Once she was finished or exhausted or both, he'd try to talk to her. To find a way to explain without explaining. To give her what he could while he held on to what was most important to him.

God, this was killing him. Just watching her as she paced in tight circles in front of him, so clearly in pain, so deeply hurt. He'd had no right, he told himself, to bring her into his messed-up life. Had no right to try to find some normalcy for himself.

He'd known from the instant he sat down beside her on that plane so long ago, that she was the one woman in the world for him. Those two weeks in Paris had given him a glimpse of what he might have if he were anybody else. And when it came time to say goodbye, he had known he couldn't do it.

The thought of living without her was so repellent,

he'd done the one thing he had always promised himself he would never do. He'd dragged an innocent person into his world. All because he hadn't been able to stand the thought of losing her.

Now, it seemed he was going to lose her anyway.

His eyes narrowed into slits as he watched the woman he loved cry. Abby never cried. She was always in control. Always smiling. Even after her mother's death, she'd held it together.

It killed him to know that *he* was the one who'd pushed her over the emotional edge. Throat dry, heart hammering in his chest, he reached for the champagne glass he'd taken from her only a few minutes ago and lifted it for a sip.

He stopped just short of his mouth when he detected a familiar scent. Frowning down at the glass, he inhaled again, just to be sure. But it was unmistakable.

Bitter almonds.

Cyanide.

Ice collected in his veins. He slanted a glance at the club, where the party was in full swing. From his vantage point, he saw at least three waiters, all of them carrying trays of drinks and appetizers. Any one of them could have given Abby the doctored drink.

Hell, maybe it had been a random attack. Not meant for any one person in particular.

Autumn moonlight shone from the sky and enveloped Abby in a silvery glow that made her seem luminescent. Despite the pain in her tear-filled eyes and the unhappy curl of her lips, she was still the most beautiful woman he had ever seen.

And if he hadn't arrived at the ball when he did, she would be dead.

Cyanide wasn't a pleasant way to die, but it was quick. Everything in him went cold and hard. Someone in that room had nearly killed his wife. The one person in the whole damn world that meant everything to him.

"Let's go," he said abruptly.

"What?" She stopped ranting, surprised at his abrupt command. "Go where?"

"Home."

"I'm not going back there with you."

"Oh, yes you are," he muttered and holding the champagne flute carefully, he grabbed her arm with his free hand and started half walking, half dragging her off the patio and down the steps to the parking area.

"Luke, let me go," she ordered, putting every ounce of her New England blue blood ancestry into her voice.

If he hadn't already been chilled to the bone, that tone would have frozen him solid. As it was, he had to get her away from here, whether she liked it or not. Whether she fought him or not. He wasn't about to stick around and give someone else a shot at killing Abby.

He stopped dead, met her furious gaze with a quelling glare and said tightly, "Abby, we're finishing this at home. You can either walk or I can throw you over my shoulder and give the parking attendants a free show. Your choice."

Stunned shock glittered in her eyes. "You're a cold bastard, Luke Talbot."

"Not the first time I've heard that."

"First chance I get," she said, her voice withering, "I'm going to make you pay for this."

"Get in line."

Then they were through talking. He tightened his grip on her elbow and took the steps at a pace that had her stumbling along in his wake. Still, he held the crystal flute carefully by its base. Didn't want to spill a drop. Didn't want to further damage any fingerprints that might be on the glass.

Damn it.

He had to find a way through this.

Had to find a way not only to convince his wife he loved her, but to keep her alive long enough to win back her trust.

Their house sat far back on a tidy, landscaped lawn. Even in the moonlight, the blooming chrysanthemums made quite a splash of color against the gray brick home. Leaded glass windows in diamond shapes lined the front rooms and a soft lamp burned behind them, sending out golden spears of light onto the lawn.

Abby swallowed hard as Luke pulled the car into the driveway. He'd driven all the way home in silence, steering one-handed and carefully holding the champagne flute in his free hand. She was grateful for the quiet between them. After all, what had been left to say? Her mind was a little blurry, her throat a little scratchy from all the ranting she'd done on the club patio and her heart was aching for all she'd lost.

Once, she'd loved this house.

When they had first bought the place, she and Luke had christened every room with their lovemaking. Sex in the living room, dining room, kitchen. Heck, she couldn't even go up the stairs without remembering herself splayed across them and Luke kneeling between her legs.

Now when she walked through the house, she felt empty. There were no sounds of children, because Luke had wanted to wait to have babies. She had gone along, wanting him to herself as long as possible, and knowing that one day, they'd begin the family they had talked about so long ago in Paris.

He turned off the engine, turned to look at her and said, "We have to talk."

"I wonder how many marriages have come to an end with those immortal words," she said, her voice a whisper.

"Abby, I don't want our marriage to end."

She turned her head to look at him and in the shadows, she told herself that there was apology in his eyes. But she knew that it was too little too late. She had loved him for so long, and so fiercely. It was hard to believe that it could all come to a shattering end.

"It's too late for that, Luke," she said and climbed out of the car, without waiting for him to open her door.

As she walked around the front of the car,

though, he was there. Waiting. And still holding her glass of champagne.

"Why'd you bring that with you?"

"I'll tell you inside."

His face was shuttered, his eyes distant and she knew it would be pointless to argue with him about it. Besides, if the truth be told, she simply didn't have the heart for another argument. She felt exhausted. Drained. All she wanted now was her bed and eight hours of oblivion.

She followed him along the walk and her heels clicked noisily against the bricks as if they were marking off the last remaining seconds of a marriage that had seemed so perfect in the beginning.

He opened the front door and stepped into the foyer. For some ridiculous reason, that solitary lamp left on in welcome made her want to cry. Welcoming them home. Probably for the last time together.

"Come into the living room," he said, as he walked across the hall, hit a light switch and entered the huge main room.

The gray brick walls looked cold and impersonal, but paintings of vivid landscapes and bright splotches of color gave life to the room. Overstuffed furniture in tones of cream and beige were artfully arranged and boasted throw pillows in jewel tones. The massive fireplace was dark and empty and a vase of freshly picked chrysanthemums spiced the air.

While she watched, Luke set the crystal flute on the mantel, then walked quickly across the gleaming hardwood floor to the front windows. There, he yanked at a cord and closed the drapes, sealing them in, shielding them from prying eyes. Better that way, Abby thought. No point in putting on a show for the neighbors.

At that thought, she almost laughed. The homes in Eastwick were so big, so far apart, she could probably scream bloody murder and no one would hear her. She could dance naked in front of the windows and no one would see her. She knew this for a fact because, once upon a time, she and Luke had tested the theory.

But that was then and this was now.

Luke turned to look at her and in his eyes, she saw something she had never seen before.

Fear.

Three

"What is it?" Abby asked, taking a half step in his direction before she realized that she shouldn't *care* what was bothering Luke.

He blew out a breath and came toward her. Abby held her ground. There were still shadows in his eyes and a firm set to his mouth that she couldn't remember ever seeing before. "There's something you have to know," he said finally.

"If this is another lie, don't bother," Abby said, guarding her heart carefully. Of course it was like locking up the house after the burglar had left with all your diamonds, but it was the intention that mattered, right?

"I haven't lied to you...exactly," he said, reaching

out and grabbing her shoulders, holding her in place in case she tried to bolt for the stairs.

"Really? So the hotel where you were supposed to be staying made a mistake when they told me they never heard of you?"

"I can explain."

"With another lie. No thank you."

"Abby something's going on here—"

"No kidding?"

"I mean," he muttered, grip tightening on her shoulders, "something more than what's happening between us."

Her heart deflated. Like a balloon in the hands of a nasty child with a pin, all of the air went out of her. "So it's not *us* you're worried about," she said flatly, surprised that the pain could keep on coming. "It's something else. Something, no doubt, way more important than our pesky little marriage."

"Damn it, will you listen to me?"

"You're not saying anything, Luke. Why should I listen?" Her gaze locked on his and she tried to see into his mind. To read the thoughts he kept hidden from her. But he was far too practiced at keeping her out. That shouldn't still have the ability to surprise her, but it did. "I don't want any more lies, Luke. I don't want you to pretend that our marriage—that *I* matter to you. I can't keep acting as if everything is wonderful between us. I can't go on living this deception."

"I *love* you, Abby," he said, "that's no deception."

His voice was no more than a breath. A hushed prayer of sound that once would have swayed her to believe everything he told her.

Now, she wouldn't allow herself that belief.

"How can I believe you?"

His shoulders slumped and his grip on her loosened just enough that she stepped out from under his touch. The fact that her skin felt cold without his hands on her meant nothing. Only that she would have to work even harder to distance herself from him.

"I'm sorry you feel that way, babe," he said at last and his voice had a thread of steel in it. "And I swear, I'll try to find a way to change your mind. But right now, there's something else you have to know."

Brush her aside and move on, was that it? *Oh, don't believe I love you? Well okay, we'll fix that later, but first...*

Suddenly exhausted, Abby felt as though she just couldn't handle one more thing thrown at her tonight. "Can't it wait until morning?"

"No."

"Fine." Resigned, she stiffened her spine. "Then tell me so I can go to bed."

"Your champagne was poisoned."

A second or two ticked past. She knew because she felt her heartbeat thudding in her chest. Luke's gaze fixed on her, Abby opened her mouth to speak, but couldn't make a sound. *Poisoned?*

"I almost drank it myself, that's when I noticed,"

Luke said, with a quick glance at the champagne flute, resting on the mantel.

In the lamplight, the wine inside the crystal looked like liquid gold. Clear. Beautiful. And, apparently, deadly.

"What?" she finally managed to say on a squeak. "You noticed what? How did you notice? Did you drink it? You didn't drink any of it, did you?" She flew at him, hands patting his shoulders, his chest, as if looking for a wound or something and even in her blind panic, she knew she was being ridiculous. If he *had* tasted the wine and it *was* poisoned, he'd be dead.

"I caught the scent of almonds just before I took a sip," Luke told her, grabbing both of her hands and holding on to them tightly. "That's cyanide, Abby. If you had drunk that champagne…if I hadn't come to the ball and taken it away from you…"

His gaze moved over her features lovingly and she felt the heat of it as surely as she would have his caress. His words filled her mind, her heart, her soul and a wild sense of dread rushed through her. "God, Luke. If you hadn't smelled the wine— How did you smell it on the wine?"

"Just lucky, I guess."

"Lucky." Yes, so very lucky, she thought. If he hadn't been so quick to notice. If he had tasted that wine. He would have died there on the patio, with the sound of her rant ringing in his ears.

And though she knew she couldn't live with him

anymore, Abby also realized she couldn't live knowing he was dead.

"How?" she asked, followed quickly by, "Why?
And who?"

"I don't know," he answered. "But I swear I'll
find out."

Cyanide?

"Someone killed my mother, Luke." Her mom,
Bunny, had diligently taken her digitalis medicine—
unaware that someone had switched those tablets for
placebos that were no help at all when she desperately needed them. Abby's gaze latched onto Luke's.
"Do you think it's the same person trying to kill me?
Or maybe not. Maybe it was an accident."

He started to talk, but she cut him off.

"No," she said quickly. "You don't *accidentally*
drop cyanide into champagne. But maybe I wasn't
the intended victim." Abby's mind filled with the
images of the crowded ballroom. Of people laughing,
talking, dancing. All of them having a good time.
Well, all but one of them. A murderer wandering
through the room with impunity.

How could she ever imagine one of the people
she'd known most of her life a cold-blooded killer?
But then, she already knew someone had murdered
her mother. Was it such a stretch to admit that that
someone was on a roll now and looking to edge up
his scorecard?

"There's no way to know if you were the intended
victim," Luke said softly.

"So it could be. Could be a mistake that I got that flute."

"Possibly," he said, but his tone said he didn't believe that.

"We should tell someone."

"We will."

"Luke…"

His hand cupped her cheek, then he speared his fingers through her hair, tugging the thick, blond mass from the diamond-studded clip. She heard it clatter onto the floor behind her and couldn't have cared less. His fingertips stroked her scalp and goose bumps raced along her spine.

"You're so beautiful, Abby," he murmured, his gaze moving over her face before locking on her eyes. He pulled in a deep breath, released it slowly and whispered, "My God, it kills me to even think about what might have happened tonight."

"Oh, me, too, Luke. Me, too." She shook her head and blinked back tears as she looked up at him.

This was a mistake.

She knew it.

But she didn't care.

If she and Luke were going to divorce, if she was never going to see him again, then she wanted tonight. She wanted to be in his arms again. Feel his body fill hers. Especially now. Now when she knew just how closely they'd both come to dying.

To losing each other forever in a way that could never be changed.

"You're everything, Abby," he whispered and bent his head to hers. A brief kiss. Featherlight. A touch of lips to lips.

And fire erupted inside her.

It had always been this way between them. A single touch was all it took to ignite the embers that were always just beneath the surface.

Then he deepened the kiss and Abby clutched at his shoulders, hanging on as her world tipped wildly. His mouth covered hers, his tongue invaded and tangled with hers while they both fought for breath.

Here was the magic, she thought, her mind clouding as sensation roared through and shut down rationality. Here was what had brought the two of them together. This was the fire that had forged them.

And no matter what else was happening in their lives, this was always good.

"I need you," he said, tearing his mouth from hers, dipping his head to kiss her throat down to the curve of her shoulder.

Abby's head fell back and she closed her eyes, concentrating on the touch of his lips against her skin. His hands moved over her, undoing the single button that held her wrap closed around her shoulders and letting the cashmere slide to the floor in an elegant heap.

Then he touched her, smoothing his palms over her arms, her back, her chest and across the tops of her breasts, displayed by the low-cut gown. Idly, he picked up the ruby pendant and held it between his fingers. Looking into her eyes, he smiled. "You wore this for me tonight."

She wanted to deny it. Hell, she hadn't even expected him to show up at the ball. But the simple truth was that he was right. She *had* worn the rubies tonight for him. As she had dressed, she had imagined his eyes on her, watching the fat ruby as it lay nestled between her breasts.

"Do you remember when I gave it to you?"

"Yes," she said on a sigh, looking into his eyes and seeing that memory reflected back on her.

"It was our first Christmas together. Christmas Eve, we sat in here, the only light in the room coming from the tree."

She swayed into him, mesmerized by his voice, by the feelings he stirred within her.

"I gave you this then because I couldn't wait for morning." His thumb stroked the cabochon stone and Abby could have sworn she felt that strong, sure touch on her skin. "You cried," he said. "You told me it was so beautiful it deserved tears."

"Luke…"

"I put it around your neck and then we made love, right here in front of the Christmas tree." He let go of the ruby and trailed his fingertips across the tops of her breasts, making her shiver. "I can still see you that night, Abby. Naked, but for the pendant, with the shine of a hundred colored lights flashing on your skin."

Her throat squeezed shut.

"And you were so beautiful," he whispered, "*you* deserved tears."

"Luke…" She fell into him, throwing her arms around his neck, clinging to him as though he were a life preserver tossed into a stormy, churning sea. She turned her face into the curve of his neck and inhaled his familiar scent. Spice and male.

His hands swept to the back of her dress and skillfully worked the zipper and the hook and eye closure at the top. When she was freed, he set her back from him and let the dress drop to the floor. His eyes popped.

"Naked?" he asked, staring at her with frenzied wonder. "You were naked under that dress? At the ball?"

She stepped out of her heels. "Couldn't have panty lines, now could I?" And she went to him as she had that first Christmas Eve, wearing only the blood-red stone he'd given her.

"I could have lost you tonight," he murmured, dipping his head to kiss her forehead, her eyes, her nose, her mouth. "I could have lost you forever."

She squeezed her eyes shut and refused to think about the sad truth. That though she had survived an attempt to kill her outright, he'd already lost her.

Still, for this one night, she would pretend. She would let go of the hurt, the pain, the betrayal and give herself over to the wonder that was Luke.

"Touch me," she said softly.

"Abby." Her name came on a groan as she pushed his tuxedo jacket off his shoulders, then quickly moved to unbutton his shirt. He tore at his belt at the same time and was pushing his slacks down and off as she divested him of the shirt and ran her palms over his broad, muscled chest.

Never ceased to amaze her, Abby thought now, hungrily exploring her husband's flesh. He looked so lean and wiry in his clothes, yet naked, the man was solid muscle. Dark brown hair matted his chest and arrowed down across a taut, flat abdomen. Her gaze dropped and her blood pressure skyrocketed. He was already hard and ready for her.

He reached out, flicking his thumbs across her hardened nipples and Abby gasped as the jolt of sensation shot through her and settled in the hot, damp core of her.

"Don't think I'm gonna be able to wait to get upstairs to the bed," he said.

"Beds are highly overrated." Abby went up on her toes, slanted her mouth across his and met his tongue with hers.

He groaned into her mouth, swept one hand down her body to the juncture of her thighs. She gasped again as he cupped her heat, working her body with his fingers until tingles of hot, demanding expectation roared into life inside her. She parted her thighs for him even as she continued to kiss him, her tongue tangling with his in a pitched battle of hunger.

One finger, then two, slipped inside her and Abby moaned, rocking her hips against his hand, needing that touch more than she needed anything else in the world.

Her body tightened, poised on the edge of completion and for that one heart-stopping moment, she wanted to freeze time. Then the moment passed in a vision-splintering explosion of sensation. Her body jolted, rocked against him and he held her tightly as his fingers brought her to a climax that nearly shattered her.

And even before the last of the tremors had eased away, he was laying her down on the closest couch, then covering her body with his.

"Gotta have you now, Abby. Now."

"Yes, Luke. *Now.*"

She hooked her legs around his middle and lifted her hips to meet him as his body plunged into hers. He filled her completely, invading not only her body, but her soul. It was always this way with Luke. He touched her more deeply than any man ever had.

His hips rocked against hers. She opened for him, sliding her arms around his neck, dragging her fingernails along his spine as he set a rhythm that she raced to follow.

Again and again, they separated only to come together again. Her body quickened again, ready for another shattering release. She held her breath and shifted beneath him, increasing the tension, the friction of flesh against flesh. And when neither of them could stand another moment of waiting, he pushed her over the edge one more time and in the next moment, let himself follow.

Only minutes later, Luke eased away from her,

picked her up and holding her close to his chest, carried her out of the room, across the foyer and up the stairs to the master bedroom.

Moonlit darkness greeted them, silver slices of light spearing through the open drapes to lie across the wide, duvet-covered bed. Luke paused only long enough to grab one end of the down quilt and toss it to the foot of the bed.

He hadn't had enough of his wife yet tonight. Doubted that he ever could. With the knowledge of the tainted champagne foremost in his mind, he felt as though he had to keep touching her, loving her, to reassure himself that she was well and with him.

The problems they had, he would find a way to iron out. He wouldn't lose her. *Couldn't* lose her.

He laid her out on the sweet-smelling sheets and took a long moment to simply look his fill. Her eyes were hazy with spent passion, her lips full from his kiss and her body limp with release. The ruby pendant lay against her skin and her blond hair spread out beneath her head on the blue sheets.

She looked like an ancient pagan goddess.

And he wanted her desperately.

Just as he had from the first moment he saw her.

"Luke…"

His name came on a sigh and the sound shuddered through him.

She lifted her arms to him and he went into her embrace like a man finding home after a long, exhausting search. Skin to skin, heat to heat, rough to smooth, their bodies lay against each other and the fire between them rekindled.

He slid down her length, taking his time, stopping along the way to nibble at her body. He took first one hardened, peaked nipple into his mouth, and then the other. He suckled her, drawing at her flesh, feeding off the soft moans of passion that slipped from her lips.

His hands moved over her body, defining every line and curve. She drew one knee up and he smiled against her breast, knowing what she wanted…needed. He slid his right hand down across her abdomen past the nest of blond curls to the heat that awaited him.

She shivered in his arms at his first touch and lifted her hips into his hand, rocking, silently demanding more. But now that the first wave of passion had been slaked, he planned to take his time. To treasure her, to stoke the fires burning within so high that neither of them would survive the inferno.

Shifting position, Luke slid off the edge of the bed, knelt on the floor and taking hold of her legs, pulled her closer. She went up on her elbows and looked at him, her hair wild, her eyes flashing with a pale blue light that never failed to leave him breathless.

He lifted her legs, draped them over his shoulders and slowly, as she watched him, lowered his mouth to her center. His gaze met hers as he tasted her. Tasted her heat, her sex. His tongue swept over the core of her, that one, tiny, sensitized nub of flesh that contained the power to send her into a frenzy of need.

She reached for him, her fingers stroking through his hair as he continued his gentle invasion. His tongue swept over her inner folds, and he felt her body jerk in response. She whimpered quietly and arched her back, tightening her grip on his hair as he worked her flesh over and over again.

"Luke, it's so good," she whispered brokenly, her heels digging into his back. "So good."

He scooped his hands beneath her, lifting her hips from the mattress, holding her tightly as she writhed beneath him. She held his head to her as if half-afraid he would stop what he was doing to her.

But he only took her higher, higher, until finally the tension in her body exploded. She screamed his name and he held her safe while the world around them shattered.

Four

Abby curled into Luke's side, her head pillowed on his chest. His arm came around her, holding her close and the sound of his heartbeat beneath her ear was both comforting and painful.

This was the last time they would be like this. The last night they would be together and her heart broke at the thought of living the rest of her life without him. Yet even as she thought it, she wondered if Luke really was the man she'd thought she knew. After all, if he had lied to her about some things, perhaps he'd lied about everything. Even down to the most basic things she'd always taken for granted. Who he was. What he was.

She closed her eyes and a single tear escaped to roll down her cheek and onto his chest.

"Abby…"

"Don't—" She stopped him, going up on one elbow to look down into his eyes. The moonlight pooled in the room, soft, incandescent. "Luke, don't say anything now. Let's just…have this night and leave the rest for morning."

He looked as though he wanted to argue. She recognized the firm set of his mouth and the slight narrowing of his dark brown eyes. But then he thought better of it, cupped her cheek in the palm of his hand. "Abby, I can guess what you're thinking about me… but you're wrong."

She let out a pent-up breath and rubbed her cheek against his palm. What felt like a cold fist tightened around her heart. "I wish that were true."

"If you'll just listen," he whispered, voice strained, eyes pleading.

She couldn't. Not now. The sting of betrayal was still too fresh. She recalled all too clearly how she had felt a few days ago, when she'd discovered that the husband she had trusted for years had lied to her about where he was. No matter what he said now, the point was, the hotel he had told her he was staying at had never heard of him.

And she couldn't forget that a woman had answered the number Luke had given her.

"I can't, Luke," she said. "I can't."

His eyes closed but not before she saw and recognized a flash of pain in their depths. She was sorry for it, but her own pain went so deep the knowledge of his brought her only a slight twinge.

Reaching out blindly for her, he wrapped his arms around her and drew her down on top of him. Holding her tightly to him, he buried his face in her hair and sighed heavily. "This is all screwed-up, Ab," he said quietly.

"I know," she answered, laying her head in the crook of his neck.

"It isn't what I wanted."

Another fresh ache rattled through her. Hardly a consolation to know that he hadn't wanted her to discover his lies.

"Please, Luke," she said, her mouth against his skin. "Don't say anything more."

His hands swept down her spine, cupped her behind and squeezed. She lifted her head, looked into his eyes and saw the fire burning there.

"If you won't let me *tell* you what I feel," he said, meeting her gaze with a steely determination that shook her to her bones. "Then all I can do is *show* you."

He flipped her over onto her back and a surprised squeak shot from her throat. He caught her chin in his hand, tipped her head back on the pillow and stared into her eyes. "I've told you before, Abby." His fingers tightened on her face. "You're *everything*."

Pushing his body into hers, he claimed her again in an ancient way. She groaned and moved with him, dancing to his rhythm again. Moving with him, opening for him, welcoming him. In this, always in this, they were in tune. They filled each other and closed off the empty places inside.

In this, they were honest.

In this, there were no lies.

"Take me," he whispered, sitting up and back onto his haunches and dragging her with him. Abby sat on his lap, impaled on his body, feeling him touch her so deeply, she thought she would never be completely alone again. "Take me, Abby. And let me take you."

She moved on him. Swiveling her hips, rocking, easing up and down on him, slowly at first, quickening the pace as their breath mingled and sighed out around them. As she moved on him, he bent his head to her breast and took her nipple into his mouth. Licking, tasting, suckling, he drove her fast and hard as she took him to the brink of oblivion.

Luke inhaled her scent, wrapped his arms tightly around her middle, holding her as closely as he could and when his release finally slammed into him, he looked into her eyes and lost himself in the blue depths that would always be *home* to him.

The next morning, Abby woke up alone.

Luke's scent was still on his pillow and her body felt limber and well used. But her husband was gone.

She sat up, looked around the room, then dropped back, disgusted, onto the bed. This shouldn't surprise her. She knew that all too well. But somehow, during those long hours of lovemaking, she'd half convinced herself that maybe their marriage wasn't over. Maybe, if they could still reach each other so completely on such an elemental level, that there was still a chance for them.

"Apparently not," she muttered into the stillness. She scooted back, and stuffed a pillow behind her, braced on the headboard. "For Pete's sake, Luke. Somebody tried to *kill* me last night. You couldn't stick around an extra hour?"

Her gaze swept the room and the only sign that Luke was back in town were his discarded clothes from last night, tossed onto a chair in the corner. Okay, maybe the cyanide hadn't been aimed at her. But the point was that she had almost drunk it! She could be dead right now. And Luke would probably *still* go into work. "Well," she whispered to the empty room, "at least I know where I stand."

Sadly, she reached out for the phone on the bedside table. Yes, it was Sunday morning, but for the amount of money she was paying her attorney, he could darn well take her call anyway.

"Louis?" she asked when a man answered.

"Mrs. Talbot?"

"Yes," Abby said, gripping the phone receiver tightly. "I know that it's Sunday, but I'd like you to have the papers delivered to my husband today."

"Today? But—"

"Please. Just do this. I already gave you his company's address. No doubt you'll find him there." One thing she could say about Luke. He was a fiend for work. He put in more hours at his job than anyone she had ever known. If he had devoted half as much energy to their marriage, this day wouldn't have come.

Her lawyer hemmed and hawed for a few seconds, then said, "A private messenger on a Sunday will be prohibitively expensive."

She didn't care.

She just wanted this over.

Her heart ached again and she rubbed her chest with her free hand as if to try to massage away the pain. It didn't help.

"It doesn't matter," Abby said. "Please, just have the papers delivered to him within the hour."

"Of course, I'll get right on it—"

"Thanks." She hung up and let her fingers rest atop the phone for a long minute, as if she could undo what she had just done. But the bottom line was, this decision had been made weeks ago. She was only following through on it now. And it would be best to have it done quickly. Then she and Luke could both move on with their lives.

Alone.

At work, Luke was haunting the lab rats—the technical geeks who can decipher any mystery once it's put on a glass slide.

"There's got to be something," he snapped, standing right behind Bernie Burkower as he huddled over the gazillion-dollar, super-duper, electron-some-thing-or-other microscope.

"Yeah," Bernie said, sitting up and pushing his

black horn-rims up higher on his sharp, beaklike nose. "There's cyanide."

"Well, I *knew* that," Luke practically snarled. He stomped around the perimeter of the lab, hardly glancing at the beakers and glass-fronted drawers and the steel tables where evidence lay spread out for examination. "What I want to know is who put it in the champagne."

Bernie's myopic gaze followed him around the room. He shrugged. "Can't tell you that, Agent Talbot. Unless it was you or your wife who did it. Yours are the only fingerprints on the crystal."

"Perfect," he muttered and stopped dead directly opposite Bernie. "I want you to go over it again. Check the rim of the base. Or the stem of the glass. You might get a partial."

Bernie gave him one of the superior looks that all of the tech guys saved for the field agents. The one that said, *If you were as smart as me, you'd be doing this job, so back off.* "I've already tested every square inch of that glass," he said tightly. "Except for yours and your wife's prints, there's nothing on it. I can run some more tests on the cyanide, maybe find unique characteristics that could lead us to possible sources."

Frustration simmered in Luke and he felt as if he were going to explode. Last night with Abby, he'd held her, loved her and today, he was finding out there was no way to be sure she was safe. If there had been fingerprints on the champagne flute, he might have been able to figure out who the intended victim was by discovering the identity of the would-be murderer. At the very least, he'd have had someone to lock up!

Turning his head to the glass wall separating the lab from the rest of the office, he looked out at his fellow agents at their desks, on the phone, surfing the Net. Everyone out there was diligently working on cases assigned to them.

Everyone but Luke.

But how the hell could he take on a new assignment when there was every chance someone was out to kill his wife?

A phone rang and Bernie stretched out one hand to grab it. "Burkower." A pause. "Right. I'll tell him."

Luke glanced at him.

Bernie hung up and shrugged. "The director wants to see you. Like now."

Scraping one hand across his face, Luke nodded, then jabbed one finger at the crystal glass still on Bernie's desk. "Check it again."

He stomped out of the lab without waiting for an answer or a smart-ass retort from Bernie. Outside the lab, the office wasn't so quiet. Keyboards clattered, telephones rang, dozens of conversations were taking place at once and from down the hall came the furious shouts of a handcuffed suspect.

To the outside world, this company was just another software developer. A leader in computer programming. Only a select few people beyond the walls of the building knew its real purpose.

Luke stalked down the long hallway, moving past cubicles, glassed-in offices and undercover agents who looked like gangbangers. He knew this world. He'd been a part of it since his senior year of college.

Recruited by a top government agency, Luke had adapted to the covert life of an operative like a chameleon. He could go from a tuxedoed guest at an embassy ball to the alleys of Hong Kong seamlessly. He became whoever he needed to become on a moment's notice.

And he loved every minute of it all.

It wasn't just the adrenaline rush of the danger and the chance to play real-life spy. It was the notion that he was doing a service for his country. Making the world a little safer for the children he hoped to have one day with Abby.

Abby.

Just short of the director's office, he stopped to pull himself together.

From the moment he'd met Abby on a plane to his Paris assignment, he had known that she was different. That she was the woman he had been born to love. And even knowing that a marriage to a civilian would be difficult, he hadn't been able to keep himself from reaching for the brass ring.

Maybe it had been selfish of him. Maybe it would have been better for her if he had walked away from what he was feeling. But he simply hadn't been able to. Life without Abby in it was no life at all.

Yet now, his marriage was crumbling, dissolving

under the mountain of half-truths he'd been forced to tell her over the years. He didn't want to be cagey with her. Wanted to be able to share everything with her.

But if he did, he would be putting her life in danger.

Still, he reminded himself, her life was already at risk. Hadn't she had a narrow escape just the night before? And who had been behind it? The same someone who had killed Abby's mom? Or was it one of Luke's enemies, trying to even a score?

God.

If he was responsible for the attack on Abby, how would he ever live with himself?

The door beside him was flung open and a tall, burly sixty-year-old man with a bald head and a bristling gray mustache glared at him. "When I send for an agent," Tom Kennedy snarled, "I mean for him to come *into* my office. Not just stand outside it staring into space."

The man turned and headed to his desk and Luke followed, closing the door behind him. A big room, as befitted the director of an agency who reported only to the President, the office was neat to the point of painful—except for the desk. Tom's desk was a vast expanse of glass and steel and the top of it was covered by files, photographs, memos, a half-eaten sandwich and a scattering of jelly beans spilling out of a tipped-over jar.

And if he had to, Tom could put his finger on absolutely anything in that pile within a heartbeat. A sort of jumbled organization.

"Sorry," Luke said to the man he'd been reporting to for eight years. "I've got some things to think about."

"You've got *plenty* to think about," Tom admonished him. "For example, your trip to Prague." He tossed a manila file to the edge of his desk, knocking a few pieces of candy to the floor. "The paperwork's all in there. Itinerary, tickets, name of your contact once you arrive. You leave in two days."

Luke picked up the folder, flipped it open, glanced at the contents, then closed it again. He ignored the quickening of his heartbeat. Hell, he always liked to start a new job. The rush. The risk. The satisfaction of getting away with something under the very noses of the guys supposed to prevent it from happening.

But today was different. Tossing the file back onto the desk, he shoved both hands into his pockets and said, "Can't do it."

"You'll be meeting with Schuman when you leave Prague for Berlin." Tom picked up a black pen, made a note on a file, then spun around in his chair and stacked it neatly on the shelf behind him.

"You're not listening," Luke said through gritted teeth. "I'm not going."

Turning back to the front, Tom kept talking. "You'll give the chip to Schuman and he'll have it coded and electronically transferred back here."

Luke had worked with the German agent many times. That wasn't a problem.

"You'll have to send someone else on this trip. Send Jackman."

Tom snorted. "Jackman doesn't speak German."

"Then send someone else."

"Check your tickets now," Tom said, leaning back in his chair and studying Luke through slitted eyes. "Make sure they're in order *before* you leave this time."

Damn it, one time. One lousy time, he'd arrived at the airport to discover that the travel arrangements made for him were with the wrong airline. He'd found a way around the situation. Just as he always had.

"I don't care if the tickets are in order, because I'm not going."

"Your flight will put you into Prague with three hours to spare before the meet."

"Damn it, Tom," Luke said, slamming both hands down onto the desk. "I told you I can't do this one."

"I heard you," the older man said, bracing his elbows on the arms of his leather chair and steepling his fingertips. "I'm just not listening."

"Well, you'd better start. I can't leave right now. Things at home are—"

"Abby?"

Luke shoved one hand through his hair and bit back a growl. "She tried to call the hotel in Sacramento direct. Naturally, they didn't have me registered there."

Tom shook his head grimly. "An oversight that won't happen again."

"It's not the point," Luke told his old friend and mentor. "The point is, Abby doesn't trust me."

"Why should she?"

"Excuse me?"

"Think about it, Luke." Tom stood, came around the desk, then perched on the corner of it. "You've been lying to her since you met. And to keep doing your job you're going to have to keep on lying to her."

"Maybe I shouldn't be doing this job anymore."

"You're too good to quit."

Luke swiveled his head to stare at his boss, his friend. "I won't lose Abby over this."

"And I'm not going to lose my best agent," Tom countered. "Look, we all make sacrifices. Marrying a civilian is tough."

"If I could tell her what I do. Why I had to lie."

Tom straightened up and shook his head. "Not an option."

Regret settled in the pit of Luke's stomach. "I know."

"You could endanger her."

"I think I already have."

Tom frowned. "The lab nerds tell me there's no way to be sure *who* was behind that cyanide drop at the party."

"I'll find out," Luke promised, his eyes narrowing, his lips thinning into a fierce, grim line. "That's why I won't be on the plane to Prague on Tuesday. I'm not leaving while Abby's in danger."

"Damn it, Jackman sucks."

Luke laughed and turned when someone knocked on the office door then opened it.

"Sorry to interrupt, sir," a young woman said, holding out a large brown envelope to Luke. "But this just came by special messenger for Agent Talbot."

Luke took it, watched the woman leave again, then ripped the envelope open. Yanking out the sheaf of papers inside, he stared at them, then lifted his gaze to Tom's.

"They're *divorce* papers. Abby's divorcing me."

Tom whistled, low and long. "Apparently, your wife doesn't want you around when she's in danger. Prague looking a little better to you now?"

Five

"I really owe you guys," Abby said and reached for her glass of chilled white wine.

"No problemo," Felicity said, after a sip of her margarita. "The Debs are ready for any emergency meeting. Right guys?"

The other women gathered around the glass-topped table nodded in solidarity. And Abby wanted to kiss each one of them.

After talking to her lawyer and arranging for Luke to get the divorce papers, she'd put in a call to Emma, looking for a little sympathy. What she had received was over and above the call of sisterhood. Emma had called everyone else and now they were all together at the Emerald Room at the country club.

They had a patio table, with a view of the pool and the lushly landscaped grounds. Pansies lined the flower beds, their bright, jewel-colored faces turned toward a watery fall sun. From the nearby tennis courts, the rhythmic slap of a ball against a racket sounded like a heartbeat. In the nearby bar, music played over the speakers and a few older men sat together arguing about their golf scores.

There was only one other patio table occupied— by two elderly women in their Sunday best, sharing tea and scones. The weather was a little cool and the wind was petulantly kicking up, but being outside assured the Debs of not being overheard.

"So," Mary said, sipping her iced tea. "What's going on, Ab?"

"Yeah," Lily asked, "what's the emergency?"

"It's Luke." Abby gripped her white wine a little tighter. She'd already sniffed at the liquid, unobtrusively checking for the scent of bitter almonds. Seemed ridiculous in the bright light of day to even consider the fact that she might have been killed the night before. But the honest truth was, it had happened—and now she was cautious. But this wine was fine. Crisp and clean and the color of sun-washed straw.

"What's wrong with him?" Mary asked, concern etched onto her features. "Is he sick?"

"No," Abby said, setting her glass down again, "but he's probably pretty furious right about now."

"Uh-oh," Felicity put in. "That doesn't sound good."

"I had him served with divorce papers today."

There. She'd said it all in one breath, rushing the words out. But hearing them said out loud gave her a cold shiver. God. She was really doing it. Really ending her marriage to a man she'd thought she would spend the rest of her life with.

Worse, a man she still loved desperately.

"Oh, girl," Emma said with sympathy, reaching across the table to pat her hand.

"It's terrible," Mary chimed in.

"Well, I can't say I'm surprised," Vanessa said softly. "You've been so sad for so long, Abby."

Tears filled her eyes but she blinked them back. They wouldn't do her any good and she certainly didn't want to give anyone at the club something new to gossip about.

Which was ironic when she stopped to think about it. Her mother had been the maven of gossip. Her column *The Eastwick Social Diary,* had detailed the goings-on in Eastwick society for eager readers all over the city.

She had lived for gossip. Not that Bunny was malicious or anything. She had just loved the scandalous idea of keeping her friends and acquaintances on their toes. Her journals were legendary—she'd written down every nugget of information, every rumor, every innuendo—which was probably why they'd been stolen by whoever killed her.

Which brought Abby right back to the danger of gossip. She didn't want other people commenting on her life, her marriage. It was bad enough that Delia

Forrester was already spinning tales about how *poor Abby* didn't have the sense to see that her own husband was cheating on her.

She winced at the thought and hunched her shoulders against unseen eyes staring at her…pitying her.

"Abby," Mary said, "are you really sure this is what you want? It's so obvious that you still love him."

"I know," she agreed sadly, tracing the tip of one finger around the rim of her glass. "And that will never change, damn it. I do love him. Always have. And, I still believe that divorcing him is the right answer, but last night…"

"Ah," Felicity whispered, "a little last-minute loving?"

"Not a little." Abby slumped back against her white wicker chair. "A *lot.*"

"Mmm…" Emma sighed heavily. "So I'm thinking that a divorce is the last thing on Luke's mind today."

"Are you really sure?" Mary asked again. "I mean, if the fire's still there, maybe it's not really over."

"It's not like I *want* to divorce him," Abby told her sincerely. "I thought when I married Luke that it was forever. We talked about having kids, building a family. But he's been stalling about the baby thing for two years now and then, to top it all off…I just discovered he's been lying to me for who knows how long and——"

"What kind of lies?"

She almost told them, but Abby couldn't quite

bring herself to confess that perhaps Delia had been right. That there was a chance that Luke was having an affair. Maybe only the latest in a long line of women he'd cheated on her with.

"Doesn't matter," she said grimly, swallowing hard past the knot of regret nearly choking her.

"It does, too," Felicity said sharply. "I always liked Luke. But if the bastard isn't treating you right, then you absolutely divorce him."

Abby smiled at her friend's quick defense.

"What about counseling?" Lily asked.

"No," Abby said softly, imagining her husband lying to whatever counselor they might see. What would be the point? "He'd never go and I don't think it would solve anything, either."

"I just hate to see it," Emma added. "You two always looked so good together."

They *had* been good. Once upon a time, they had been the best. But that felt so long ago now, Abby could hardly remember that sharp blade of happiness. There had once been a time when they could look into each other's eyes and know what the other was feeling.

But there had also been a time when Luke could tell Abby where he would be on a business trip and Abby could believe him. That ship had clearly sailed. Anger twisted together with pain inside her and she sighed again at how badly her life was turning out. Here it was, a lovely Sunday afternoon, when she and Luke could have been cozied up at home together, but instead, Abby was here with her friends and Luke…

"Oh, God," Abby said on a groan, "I had them deliver the divorce papers to his office."

"Ouch," Lily said.

"Hey," Mary retorted, looking from one woman to the next, "we're on Abby's side, remember."

"Oh, no doubt." Felicity lifted her glass. "We're here for you, Ab," she said, waiting for the others to join in her toast. "No matter what. You need us, we're here."

The tightness in her chest hadn't eased a bit, but somehow, the knot in her throat was dissolving. Yes, she was losing her husband. Something she might never recover from, emotionally. But she still had her friends. That said, maybe she wasn't as completely alone as she'd thought she was.

Luke was waiting for her when she walked in.

Divorce papers rolled up and gripped tight in one fisted hand, he slapped them against his thigh as if to remind himself why he was damn mad.

He heard the door open, heard her drop her keys onto the hall table. The wall clock behind him ticked loudly in the silence. Sunlight poured in through the diamond-shaped leaded windows and shone on the tables that gleamed with the lemon polish that scented the air. He listened to the click of her heels as she walked across the foyer headed for the living room and his gaze locked on the open doorway.

Her eyes widened and she sucked in a gulp of air.

"Surprised to see me?" he asked, silently congratulating himself on the calm, even tone of his voice.

"I thought you were at work."

"It's Sunday. We used to spend Sundays together."

"We used to do a lot of things," she said and started to back out of the room, clearly trying to avoid any kind of confrontation.

He wasn't going to let her.

"Like talk?" he asked.

"Yes."

He nodded, and tossed the furled divorce papers onto the coffee table, but kept his gaze locked on her. "So you mean, in the old days, you would have actually *told* me before serving me with divorce papers?"

Abby winced and it gave him no pleasure. But instead of stepping back into the hall, she came forward into the living room. "In the old days, there wouldn't have *been* divorce papers."

"I can't believe you're doing this, Abby."

He hadn't wanted to let her know just how deep the hurt went. But damn it, how was a man supposed to cover that up? Luke looked at her and felt the swell of love rushing to compete with the ache centered around his heart. He'd known that she wasn't happy.

But he hadn't known she was unhappy enough to walk out on him. And whether it was right or not, a sense of betrayal settled over him. Last night, when they were together, he'd felt all the jagged pieces of his soul fall back into place. As if the fight with Abby had never happened. As if they were still as they'd once been.

They had rediscovered the passion that had drawn

them together in the first place. They'd reconnected in a basic, elemental way. And Luke had convinced himself that they would find a way past their present problems—only to find out that Abby had secretly been planning to divorce him.

Cut a man's legs out from under him.

Add that to the fear still chewing at him—he hadn't forgotten that Abby's life had been threatened the night before—and he was in no mood to be reasonable.

"I *have* to do this, Luke," Abby said, laying one hand on her chest as if trying to hold her heart in place. "I have no choice."

"There's always a choice."

"No. Not for me." She shook her head fiercely and her blond hair flew wildly about her head. "I can't keep living this half life."

"Half life? What the hell does that mean?" He jammed both hands into his pockets and fisted them helplessly.

"It's what we have, Luke," she cried and this time her voice broke, chipping away at his heart at the same time. "I live here—you live…God. I don't even know where. What I do know is you don't live here. With me."

"This is crazy."

"No it's not," she insisted and a solitary tear escaped her eye and rolled down her cheek. "This house is no more than a place to store your stuff. You check in from time to time, but you're never really *here*."

Pain slapped at him again and Luke wanted to

argue with her. Hard to do, though, considering she was too close to the truth. "Abby…"

"Even when we're in the same room together, your mind is somewhere else, Luke." She moved to stand behind one of the twin sofas, keeping its bulk between them. Her hands gripped the chenille fabric until her knuckles whitened. "I can't keep being a part-time wife, Luke. I want the marriage we should have had. I want the babies we used to talk about. I want—"

His throat tight, he managed to say, "Go ahead. You want what?"

Her gaze locked on his and he felt the pain shining there as deeply as he felt his own.

"Mostly, I want to be able to trust my husband. And I don't."

He opened his mouth to combat that charge, but she rushed on quickly.

"No," she said, lifting one hand to keep him quiet. "You wanted to hear this, so I'm going to say it. I don't trust you anymore, Luke. You lied to me. And if you lied this time, you've probably been lying to me for years. You weren't at the hotel where you said you were going to be. And that *woman* answered when I dialed the phone number you gave me."

"I can ex—"

"I won't stay with a man who thinks so little of me that he's off having affairs with God knows how many women. I won't do it."

"Affairs?" Insult stung sharply. Over the years, he'd been away on more assignments for the government than he could count. He'd had to pretend to be married a couple of times for covert ops and he'd even had to pick up women in bars or kiss someone to keep his cover intact. But never once had he *ever* considered cheating on the only woman he'd ever loved. "I've never cheated on you, Abby."

"Oh." She drew her head back, gave him a wide-eyed look of feigned happiness and added, "You didn't? Well, why didn't you say so? Then sure. Everything's okay now. I believe you."

"Damn it."

"No," she countered quickly, hotly. "You're not going to talk your way out of this, Luke. I know something's going on. I know you're lying to me and the only thing that makes any sense of this at all is that you're a cheating husband."

"That's great," he snapped and before she could back up, stalked around the edge of the couch and grabbed hold of her shoulders. "That's just perfect. You're supposed to be the one person in the world who knows me better than anyone else. And you seriously believe I would cheat on you?"

Her head fell back and she looked up at him. Luke saw the sheen of tears in her eyes and wanted to do whatever he had to, to wipe them away. But damn it, he didn't know what he *could* do. He was sworn to secrecy about his job and even though his marriage—the only truly sacred thing to him in his life—was on the line, he didn't have the right to disregard the vow he'd made to his country.

"I don't want to believe it," Abby said, her gaze locked with his. "But what choice do I have, Luke?"

His fingers dug into her shoulders and only loosened slightly when she winced and he realized he was hurting her. "Abby, when we met in Paris, I told you that I had to travel. A lot. For my job. I didn't lie to you about that. You knew going in what it would be like."

"And in Paris," she countered, "we talked about having a family. Remember that, Luke? We wanted three kids. We even named them."

He did remember. Lying beside Abby on a narrow bed in a splash of moonlight, they'd laid out their plans for their life together. And Luke, even knowing that his job with the agency was going to make a normal life tough to manage, had wanted it all as badly as she had.

Now it was his turn to wince.

"But," she said softly, sadly, "every time I bring up the subject of us having a baby, you shut me down. You say, 'in a few months, babe'…or, 'next year, babe, when things slow down at work.'"

Luke sighed, knowing she was right and wishing she weren't. "It's not that I don't want kids. Of course I want kids with you, Abby…"

She shook her head. "It's not just that, Luke, at least not that alone. It's everything. Yes, you travel, but now I know you don't always tell me where you really are."

"I want to tell you, Abby," he admitted. "I just—
can't."

She laughed shortly, humorlessly. "That's great. You've made my point for me, Luke. You don't trust me. And I won't live with a man I can't trust."

The phone rang and though Luke would have ignored it, Abby made a beeline for it, as if grateful for the interruption.

"Hello?" She frowned, disgusted, before saying, "I don't know why you keep calling here. I've told you over and over again, there is no Lucy living here."

She hung up and shook her head. "At least once a month, some man calls for *Lucy*. Doesn't matter how often I tell them they've got the wrong number, someone's always looking for that woman. She must be really popular."

Luke was hardly listening. *Lucy* was the code name the agency used to call him into the office. But, he told himself, since Abby was clearly more suspicious than she ever had been before, looked like they were going to have to change the protocol.

The phone rang again a split second later and this time, Luke grabbed it before Abby could. "Hello?"

"You know," Bernie Burkower grumbled, "you could answer the phone yourself sometimes so I wouldn't have to listen to your wife yell at me."

"Yes, I understand," Luke hedged, smiling and nodding at Abby while she watched him.

"She's standing right there, isn't she?" Bernie asked.

"That's right."

"Well, this could be fun," Bernie continued. "What's she wearing?"

Perfect. Luke was straddling a bottomless canyon filled with danger and Bernie wanted to make jokes. When he got back to the office, first thing he was going to do was punch him dead in the nose. Luke's hand tightened on the receiver. "I'll get right on it."

"Not gonna tell me?" Bernie whined.

"Who is it?" Abby asked.

"The office," Luke told her, then to Bernie, said tightly, "You have something for me?"

"Fine. If you're not going to cooperate, back to business then," the other man complained. "Yeah, I'm finished running the champagne and the glass."

"And…?"

"I might have found something with the cyanide."

A cold chill crawled along his spine. He glanced at Abby and she looked so beautiful and vital and so damn *alive* in the sunlight that outlined her body like a halo—it was impossible to believe that she'd come so close to dying only the night before.

"What do they want?" Abby asked, stepping closer. Sunlight scattered over her hair like liquid gold and glittered in her still-tear-filled eyes.

He couldn't tell her what was going on, yet for the first time in his marriage, he was sorely tempted to confess everything.

His wife?

Or his country?

And why the hell did it have to be one or the other?

"I'm going to have to go in again," Luke told her

and watched her determinedly blink back the tears until her eyes were cold and dry.

"If you're coming in, why am I still on the phone?" Bernie demanded.

"No reason," Luke said sharply and hung up, with Bernie still babbling.

"You're going into work," Abby said. "In the middle of—"

"You know what you said earlier about having no choice?" Luke asked. "Well, this time, neither do I."

"You said there was always a choice."

"I was wrong."

He had to find out everything Bernie knew. Had to figure out who had tried to kill Abby before they tried again. God, he'd always imagined that he'd been able to strike a real balance between his secret agent life and his home life. But apparently, he'd been fooling himself. Not only was his marriage dissolving around him, but while he had been out saving the world, someone was trying to kill his wife.

"It's okay, Luke. I was wrong, too," Abby said softly and reached out as if to touch his cheek. Then, before she made contact, she let her hand drop to her side. "About a lot of things."

Six

Abby could actually *see* Luke withdraw.

He was standing a mere foot from her but he might as well have been on the moon. It didn't matter that they were in the middle of dissecting their marriage. His focus had clearly shifted to whatever was happening at the office.

Obviously the computer software business was far more fascinating than she would have guessed.

When Luke hung up the phone Abby waited to hear what had been so darn fascinating that he was willing to walk away from their most important conversation to go back to work.

"Abby," he finally said, "this morning, while you

were still sleeping, I took that champagne glass to a lab."

"What lab?" she asked.

"Doesn't matter," he answered quickly. "I've uh, got an old friend who works at a top-of-the-line facility. He ran some tests for me."

He.

Was he telling the truth? Or was this yet another lie?

"And…?"

"And I was right. The champagne was doctored."

She swallowed hard. "Cyanide."

"Yeah."

It felt as if all the air had been sucked from her lungs. Okay sure, she'd been living with the information since the night before, when Luke had told her his suspicions. But this was confirmation. She'd blithely accepted a flute of champagne from a passing waiter and if Luke hadn't shown up, she would have died right there at the country club ball.

Sinking onto the couch behind her, Abby lifted one hand and covered her mouth.

Luke took a seat on the coffee table in front of her. He tossed the phone onto a sofa cushion, then took both of her hands in his. "My friend says the only prints on the glass were yours and mine. I want you to think back. When you got that champagne, did the waiter hand it to you?"

That moment popped into her mind and she was there again, surrounded by people and feeling so alone. She heard the music, felt the wind off the terrace and heard the waiter saying, "Ma'am? More champagne?"

"He offered it to me a couple of times," she murmured, remembering it all so clearly. "At first, I wasn't paying attention and then…" Her gaze met Luke's. "No, he didn't hand it to me. I took it off the tray."

"Was there more than one glass on the tray?"

His eyes were steely, his voice a slash of low-pitched sound filled with determination.

"Why is that important?"

"If there was more than one, if this waiter, whoever he was, was offering you a choice, then the poisoning was random. Could have been meant for anyone."

God.

The poisoning.

"No," she said, shaking her head, but keeping her gaze locked with his. "There was only one glass. I remember thinking that everyone must be having a great time, because the champagne was really moving."

Abby laughed shortly, a painful scrape in her throat and Luke's hands tightened on hers.

"Someone tried to kill me," she whispered.

He nodded. "Looking that way."

"But why?" It was a question that had no answer, but it was one she couldn't shake.

"That's what we have to find out," he told her, lifting his hands to cup her face. "And we *will* find out, Abby. I swear it."

It felt so good to have his hands on her. To feel

the warmth of his skin on hers. To savor the connection that always flared into life between them. But a part of her knew that it was foolish to take comfort here. Because Luke wasn't going to be a part of her life anymore. Allowing herself to lean on him, depend on him, would only stretch out the pain of their eventual split.

Because nothing had really changed.

Despite everything else going on around them, the painful truth was that she couldn't trust Luke anymore. And though her heart was breaking, she knew she had to defend against further pain.

She pulled back, away from his touch, and fought her instinct to move in close again. "Luke, I appreciate your help—and believe me when I say I'll accept all the help I can get to figure out what's going on."

"I hear a *but* in there."

"But," she said nodding, "I haven't changed my mind about the divorce."

"Damn it, Abby, if you think I'm going to leave you while—"

"I'm perfectly safe in my own home," she said, interrupting him quickly. At least, she *hoped* she was safe here. She'd hate to think that she was in danger in the home she loved so much. "And I don't think it's a good idea for you to continue living here."

"Tough."

"Excuse me?"

"I said tough." Luke leaned back on the table, but his hard, unforgiving gaze met hers and she knew he wasn't going to budge an inch on this. "I'm not going anywhere."

"Luke, our marriage is—"

"The marriage and divorce talk can wait, Abby." He stood, looked down at her and said, "I'm not leaving you. Not when there's somebody after you. Not until I know you'll be safe."

But who, she wondered, would keep her safe from *him?* If he stayed, if they spent more time together, it would only make their eventual parting more painful. And as it was, the pain was staggering.

"Luke," she said, standing, too, to meet him on a more or less equal basis. Even though she had to look up to stare into his eyes. "What happened between us last night—that won't be happening again."

"Fine." His jaw tight, his mouth a grim slash, he looked at her. "You don't want me in your bed, that's your choice and I'll respect it. You want me to leave you to face danger on your own and I'll fight you on it."

Her heartbeat quickened as she heard the tension in his voice and sensed it pouring off him in thick waves. She wished she could believe his feelings were based on the love she'd once counted on so completely.

"I have to get into the office," he said abruptly and checked his wristwatch. "Shouldn't be more than an hour. So get ready for some conversation when I get back. We're going to find a way to get to the bottom of this, Abby. Whether you want me in this with you or not…you're stuck with me."

* * *

Luke went directly to his supervisor.

"Tom, I need a leave of absence. A few days—" He caught himself, shook his head and admitted, "Maybe more. I can't leave Abby alone until I find out what's going on. She was almost poisoned last night."

The big man sighed and leaned back in his chair. Grimly, he studied Luke for a long minute before saying, "This is going to put us in a bind. We already went over this. We need you in Prague."

"Anyone can make that connection. Only *I* can keep Abby safe."

"You know, I could arrange for someone to keep an eye on your wife while you go on this mission."

Luke shook his head. "No. I'm not leaving her. But," he added, "I'll take you up on the extra eyes. I'd like to get one of the guys to follow her during the day. Keep her safe when I'm not with her."

"I'd want the same thing for my wife if I was in your shoes. You pick the agent you want as your wife's tail. I'll take care of the rest." Sitting up straight, Tom reached for his desk phone, punched in a set of numbers and muttered grimly, "Find Jackman. Tell him he's going to Prague."

Relief shot through Luke. He'd still have duties around this office, but he wouldn't be out of the country. Plus he'd be able to get one of his friends to watch over Abby when he couldn't. And he'd be at her side every night. Whether she wanted him there or not.

When Tom hung up, he grimaced. "Good thing

Schuman speaks English. Jackman's German wouldn't get him a cup of coffee."

"I owe you, Tom."

"Damn straight you owe me," the other man said, waving one beefy hand in dismissal. "Get this thing with your wife straightened out so you can get back to work."

"Oh," Luke promised him, "I'll get this situation sorted out. Fast. *Nobody* threatens my wife."

The next night over dinner, conversation was strained. In the old days, Abby used to love having this hour with her husband. They had a chance to talk. To share the events of their day. To laugh together.

Now, however, there were too many shadows in the room for them to pretend that they were easy with each other anymore. They were eating in the huge, farmhouse style kitchen. A round pedestal table sat before a bay window where potted herbs thrived on glass shelves. The sunshine-yellow walls shone in the lamplight, but outside the windows, the darkness crouched.

"It's good," Luke said, breaking the silence that had seemed thick enough to slice. "Always did like your lasagna."

Abby forced a smile that felt stiff and she wondered if he noticed. "Thanks. I needed something complicated today. Something to keep my mind off—" *You*, she added mentally.

"You didn't go to work?" he asked.

"No." She'd called in sick, something she never

would have done even a year ago. But these days, she didn't feel like going into work and was seriously considering just giving notice and walking away. And that was part of the problem lately, too, she admitted. Her job contributed to the dissatisfied feeling that was so much a part of her lately.

Not so very long ago, she had loved going into work. Loved being an executive at a perfume company. It was exciting to be in on the marketing decisions. To be listened to and respected when she made suggestions. She used to enjoy sitting behind her desk, talking to clients on the phone, going to lunch with the company president and discussing strategic plans for the future.

But in the last year, her job—like her marriage— had lost its shine. She felt as though there were other things she could be doing. Other, more fulfilling things. Maybe she could try painting. Or writing.

Or, being a mother?

In her heart of hearts, she admitted that what she wanted most was children. She and Luke had always talked about them. Although now, the chances of that happening were slim to none.

Pain, old and familiar, rippled through her and she shut down that train of thought because she simply couldn't bear to think about it anymore.

"Have you found out anything else about the champagne?" she asked, the silence in the room, her own thoughts forcing her to speak or deal with emotions she didn't want to face.

"Nothing that I haven't already told you."

Both of her eyebrows lifted in question.

"I *mean* it," he said gruffly. "I told you what I know about the damn champagne and the glass it was in. There's just nothing."

"That doesn't make me feel any better."

"It shouldn't. Something's going on here in Eastwick. And nobody's going to be safe until we figure it out."

Abby picked up her glass and drank a healthy gulp of wine. It didn't help to settle her suddenly tumbling stomach, but it did ease the dryness in her throat. "Do you think this all has something to do with my mother's murder?"

"Possibly." He watched her and Abby felt her own tension ease a little at the steadiness in his gaze. Funny that just having him close was comforting. Especially when she'd claimed not to want him around.

"Did you tell me everything you know about Bunny's death?"

"Yes," she said, still holding on to her wineglass as if it were a life preserver. She stared down into the deep red liquid as if looking for answers she would never find and said, "The pills she thought were her digitalis were really placebos." She tried very hard not to think about her mother suffering, in pain, futilely waiting for her pills to ease the strain on her heart. "*Someone* switched those pills. But the police don't have any ideas. No leads. No suspects."

"None?" he asked, and for the first time a wry smile curved one corner of his mouth.

She gave him a half smile in return. "Okay, touché. The problem is, not that there are *no* suspects, but that there are too *many* suspects in Mom's death. The killer could have been any number of people she wrote about in her column."

"Have to give Bunny credit," Luke mused wryly. "She knew more about dishing dirt than a land-scape designer."

"Yeah, she did." Her mother hadn't always been popular with the people who appeared in her columns, but Abby had loved her deeply. And most of her friends had been very sweet since Bunny's death. Only one or two people had even hinted at being more relieved than grieved at Bunny's passing. As that thought settled in, she spoke up. "You know, there was something else."

His gaze sharpened. "What?"

"It's probably nothing, but not long after Mom died, Frank Forrester said something that I didn't think anything of at the time."

"But now…"

"Now, I don't know."

"Tell me."

His eyes were so dark they were nearly black and he was so focused on her that Abby had to fight the urge to fidget. "It's probably nothing," she hedged, feeling a little foolish now for even mentioning it, but the more she thought about it, the more she wondered.

"Just tell me."

"Right. Okay, I forget where we were," she said, going back in her mind now to try to pull up the correct memory, "probably at the club, though. Yeah." She brightened up, gave him a smile and said, "It was a Debs lunch at the club. I got up to get another drink from Harry, the bartender, and Frank was there, getting a refill for some of his golfing cronies."

"Frank?"

"Yes. He told me how sorry he was about Mom, and then he said that not too long ago, he'd had a close call of his own with his digitalis." She frowned. "He said something vague about a screwup with his dosage or something. Then he mentioned he's now put Delia in charge of his medication."

"Scary thought," Luke said.

"Totally." Abby smiled, recalling how many times she and Luke had admitted that they found Delia Forrester cold and a little intimidating. And just for a second or two, it was good between she and Luke again. Easy. As it used to be. The two of them enjoying sharing the same thoughts and sense of humor. But that moment passed all too quickly.

"I'll check into it," Luke said. "See what I can find out about Frank's close call and—"

"How're you going to do that?" Abby asked, frowning. "You're not with the police, Luke. People aren't going to tell you anything."

He swallowed hard and mumbled something about a *friend* he could call on for help.

"Who is this friend?"

"No one you know."

"Perfect," Abby said and took another sip of wine as the sigh of disappointment washed over her. "Even more secrets."

"Abby…"

"No, never mind." God, she didn't want to talk about it again. Didn't want to rehash everything they'd already said. Especially didn't want to hear more of Luke's lies. "Let's just drop it, okay?"

"Okay." Luke took a relieved breath and changed the subject entirely. "What's new in the perfume business?"

Abby looked at him for a long moment. "You don't really care, do you?"

"Of course I care. What's important to you is important to me."

"I wish I could believe that." It tore at her that she couldn't. Couldn't believe anything he said, really. He'd lied to her so well, so completely, how would she ever know truth from lie?

He blew out a breath and picked up his wineglass. Taking a sip of the dark, rich burgundy, he set the glass back down and said quietly, "Okay, so we won't talk about work."

"We can talk about *your* work," she said, eyeing him. "For example, when's the next 'business' trip?"

His gaze snapped to hers. "I was supposed to leave tomorrow."

"Supposed to?"

"I'm not going." He took another bite of lasagna and talked around it. "Told the boss to send someone else."

"You shouldn't have done that."

"Why the hell not?"

"Because I don't want you here," Abby said flatly and wondered if he knew that for the lie it really was. Could telling lies make you an expert at *identifying* them? Another interesting question she supposed she'd never get an answer to. "I think you should move out. I filed for divorce, in case you've forgotten."

His fork dropped onto the plate with a clatter that made her wince.

"Not likely to forget that," he assured her. "It isn't every day that a man gets served with divorce papers at the office."

"I—" she held up both hands "—I just wanted it over with. Done and over."

"What's between us will *never* be over, Abby."

"Don't, Luke. Don't do this. Don't make this harder on both of us than it has to be." She stood, carrying her plate to the sink.

He was right behind her, so quickly she hardly heard him move. Grabbing hold of her, he spun her around and pulled her so close to him she had to tip her head back to meet dark eyes filled with fury.

"It *should* be hard, Ab," he said through gritted teeth. "Ending our marriage should be damn near impossible. Why would I want to make it easy for you?"

"Why are you so determined to hold on?"

"Because I *love* you."

Abby's heart twisted in her chest and air was suddenly hard to come by. The ring of truth sounded in his voice, but what did that mean? She'd been fooled before.

Besides, now that she knew their bond was so fragile, love simply wasn't enough. She needed to know he trusted her. Needed to know…oh God, she needed to know *she* could trust *him*.

His grip on her loosened as the expression on his features softened. Sliding his hands up and down her arms, stroking her skin as if trying somehow to soothe her, he whispered, "Abby, I never cheated on you. Never."

Tears stung her eyes and his image wavered and blurred. She wanted to believe him—more than she'd ever wanted anything. But how could she? Hadn't she herself caught him in a lie? Hadn't a woman answered the phone when she called him on his last business trip?

"Please, Abby," he said, his voice a caress. "Believe me."

"I want to," she admitted, which was more than she had intended to say. "But to do that, you have to tell me the truth. What's going on with you? Where were you *really* on that last trip? Who was the woman who answered the phone pretending to be a hotel operator?"

"If I could tell you, don't you think I would?"

"I think you've been lying to me for so long now, it's become second nature."

Several long seconds ticked past and she held her breath, hoping, waiting. Unreadable emotions flashed across his eyes and his jaw worked as though he was literally biting back the words that were fighting to get out. Finally, though, he dropped his forehead to hers.

"Babe, I wish I could tell you what you want to know. You have no idea how badly I wish it," he said, voice hard-edged, steely. "But I can't. I'm sorry."

Abby's eyes closed tightly, briefly. His hands on her arms were warm and familiar, but that warmth didn't negate the cold creeping through her bones. Regret choked her and she had to fight for breath. She hadn't known she could still feel fresh pain. But it seemed that there was always more.

When she opened her eyes, she stepped away from the man she'd once thought she knew better than anyone. She needed that distance between them. Needed a physical reminder that what they'd once had was long over. That there was no going back.

As long as he insisted on keeping her in the dark.

"I'm sorry, too, Luke," she said and turned away from him. She flipped up the stainless steel lever over the faucet and watched as a rush of hot water splashed into the sink. "Now, if you won't leave the house, then you can at least move into the guest room."

"Abby, whatever you're thinking, we're still married."

"Not for long," she said firmly, despite the sheen of tears blurring her vision. "I can't be married to a

man I don't trust, Luke. More, I *won't* be married to
a man who doesn't trust me or respect me enough to
tell me the truth."

Seven

Over the next few days, Luke and Abby reached a sort of armed truce.

At least, that's how she thought of it. He stayed in the house, but he slept in the guest room, just next door to the master bedroom. Abby had thought that if he were in another room, it would make this whole situation easier.

It didn't.

She lay awake every night, listening to him prowl the confines of his own room. She wondered what he was thinking, why he was so restless. And she wondered if he was spending as much time thinking about her as she was thinking about him.

The nights seemed to last forever, but the days

flew past. She tried to keep as busy as possible. She even went into work and did her best to focus on the tasks at hand. But it was nearly impossible.

She'd blown a meeting with a prospective client and then had forgotten to call another one back. So much for being the dedicated executive. If she didn't quit soon, Abby had the distinct impression she might be fired.

This is what her world had come to.

But how was she supposed to be concerned with next year's perfumes when there were so many other things—more important things—to obsess about?

The attempt on her life.

Her mother's murder.

Luke.

"And that's the bottom line, ladies and gentlemen," she murmured, throwing back the blanket and jumping out of bed. She couldn't think because Luke was occupying all of her thoughts.

Clearly, even divorce wasn't going to be enough to get him out of her mind. Her heart.

She walked across the big room, the plush, pale blue carpet soft beneath her bare feet. At the French doors leading to the stone terrace, she stopped, pulled back the sheer drapes and stared out into the night.

"Bottom line," she whispered into the silence, "I still love him. Always have. Always will."

Her grip on the curtains tightened until she deliberately relaxed her grip and smoothed the creases in the fabric.

Fine. She loved her husband.

A man she *knew* was lying to her.

A man she *suspected* was cheating on her.

How had it all come to this? They'd started out so well. So happy. So perfectly matched. It was as if they'd been made for each other.

Now, Abby wasn't sure of anything anymore.

As she stood there in the shadows, she heard a voice. Muffled, but distinct. Frowning, she moved to the wall separating her room from Luke's. Leaning in, she put her ear to the wallpaper, closed her eyes and listened intently.

"No," he said clearly, then there were a few words she missed, followed by, "take out."

Take out? She pulled her head back, stared at the wall as if she had X-ray vision or something and then instantly put her ear back against the wall. She held her breath and strained to hear more.

"Follow *mumble mumble mumble* tail and don't *mumble mumble mumble* her."

"Oh for heaven's sake," she muttered, frustrated and more intrigued than ever.

"Counting *mumble* you to *mumble* cover her *mumble mumble* until *mumble mumble.*"

Gritting her teeth, Abby realized she'd never hear well enough through the stupid wall. Following her instincts, she moved quietly across the room, eased the door open and stepped out into the hall. A draft skittered past her and sent goose bumps racing up and down her spine.

This was just perfect. She'd been reduced to sneaking around her own house in the middle of the night to listen in on her husband's phone conversations. She had actually become the betrayed wife in every old movie she had ever seen. All she needed to do to complete the picture was hire some hard-boiled private detective to follow Luke around and snap blurry pictures.

Hmm. She tilted her head to one side and seriously considered it. For a half second or so. Then she dismissed it and tiptoed to the guest-room door. Bracing both hands on the doorjamb, Abby *very* carefully swung her hair out of the way and then gently placed her ear against the wood panel.

His voice was a little clearer here, she thought with an inward smile of victory. Now maybe she'd get some answers. Maybe she'd actually hear him talking to whatever woman he was cheating with.

Abby winced and closed her eyes. Did she really want to hear Luke talking to another woman? No. Was she determined to? Yes.

Swallowing back her distaste for the whole situation, Abby held her breath and listened.

"I don't care," Luke said. "I told you this is important to me. You have to understand that I'm not going to leave until I get what I'm after."

Her breath left her in a rush. *What he's after?*

"You do this my way, Katherine."

Abby muffled a groan. The bitch had a name. And

a nice name at that. Why couldn't she have been a Bambi or a Musty or something?

"All you have to do is stay out of sight, damn it. How hard is that?"

She leaned in closer to the door, tears brimming in her eyes even as she strained to hear more.

Luke's voice dropped and Abby frowned tightly. Darn it. She hadn't heard enough. He couldn't hang up. Not yet.

The door flew open and, unbalanced, Abby fell into the room, bounced off Luke's bare chest and stumbled backward into a table, knocking the Tiffany lamp to the floor with a shattering crash.

"Damn it, Abby, watch out," he shouted as she backed away from him.

"Me?" She slapped one hand to her chest. "I should look out? You better watch your own step, buddy boy."

"Buddy boy?"

Abby held out one hand, palm up, to keep him at bay. She couldn't let him touch her. Wouldn't let him near her. "*Katherine* probably wouldn't want you getting too chummy with me, now would she?"

"Kath—" Clearly disgusted, he tossed the cordless phone onto the bed. "You were listening."

"Damn straight I was and, hey, I got an earful." Her anger propelled her into the room.

"Abby, you don't understand—" He broke off and shouted, "Stop!"

"No— OW!" She stepped on a shard of glass and

before she could even slump with the pain, Luke was there, scooping her up into his arms.

Physical pain radiated up her leg, but emotional pain far outweighed everything else. She pushed at his chest, her hands skidding across his chest and not budging him one bit. The man might look lean, but every inch of him was solid muscle.

"Put me down."

"Right. Put you down so you can walk barefoot through broken glass some more. Great idea." He tightened his grip on her, stalked into the attached bathroom.

"I'm serious, Luke," she said as he plopped her butt down onto the green granite counter. "I don't want you to even touch me."

"Tough." He grabbed her bleeding foot, swung her around so that it was in the sink, then turned on the water.

"That hurts!" She struggled in his grip, but she might as well have tried to push at a mountain. The man had no intention of letting her go. "Turn it off."

He shot her a furious glare and snapped, "Shut up, Abby."

"Shut up? You're telling me to— OW!" She slapped his shoulder, hard, but couldn't make him stop his ministrations. And to give him his due, his big hands were gentle on her foot as he carefully pulled out the small piece of glass and threw it into the trash can. Then, holding her steady, he kept her foot under the stream of warm water until the bleeding eased a bit.

GET FREE BOOKS and FREE GIFTS WHEN YOU PLAY THE...

Lucky 7

SLOT MACHINE GAME!

Just scratch off the silver box with a coin. Then check below to see the gifts you get!

YES!

I have scratched off the silver box. Please send me the 2 free Silhouette Desire® books and 2 free gifts for which I qualify. I understand I am under no obligation to purchase any books, as explained on the back of this card.

326 SDL EF4H   **225 SDL EF4A**

FIRST NAME	LAST NAME

ADDRESS

APT.#	CITY

STATE / PROV.	ZIP/POSTAL CODE

7	7	7	**Worth TWO FREE BOOKS plus 2 BONUS Mystery Gifts!**
🍒	🍒	🍒	**Worth TWO FREE BOOKS!**
♣	♣	♣	**Worth ONE FREE BOOK!**
🔔	🔔	🍒	**TRY AGAIN!**

www.eHarlequin.com

(S-D-10/06)

The Silhouette Reader Service™ — Here's how it works:

Accepting your 2 free books and 2 free mystery gifts places you under no obligation to buy anything. You may keep the books and gifts and return the shipping statement marked "cancel." If you do not cancel, about a month later we'll send you 6 additional books and bill you just $3.80 each in the U.S., or $4.47 each in Canada, plus 25¢ shipping and handling per book and applicable taxes if any.* That's the complete price and — compared to cover prices of $4.50 each in the U.S. and $5.25 each in Canada — it's quite a bargain! You may cancel at any time, but if you choose to continue, every month we'll send you 6 more books, which you may either purchase at the discount price or return to us and cancel your subscription.

*Terms and prices subject to change without notice. Sales tax applicable in N.Y. Canadian residents will be charged applicable provincial taxes and GST. All orders subject to approval. Credit or debit balances in a customer's account(s) may be offset by any other outstanding balance owed by or to the customer. Please allow 4 to 6 weeks for delivery.

Finally, he shut off the water, grabbed a hand towel from the nearby stainless steel ring and pressed it to the bottom of her foot.

"Not that towel, it's—" She blew out a breath. "Never mind."

"Hold this in place till I get back."

"Back? Where are you going?"

"To clean up the rest of the broken lamp before you slice off your leg."

She gave him a dismissive smirk. "Very amusing."

"Nothing about this is amusing, Abby. Now hold that towel against your foot with steady pressure."

Abby's nightgown was hiked up her thighs and her bottom was icy cold, sitting on the darn granite. The harsh overhead light shone down on Luke, creating shadows on his rugged face that made him look a little more dangerous than she could ever remember seeing him. Funny how a trick of the light could make her calm, sweet-natured husband look like the Terminator.

"You have no right to give me orders," she said, but held on to the towel anyway.

"Seems like I just gave you one. So do it."

"Or what?"

Muffling a tight growl of fury, he leaned in close, braced both hands on either side of her and glared directly into her eyes. "Don't push me, Ab."

"Fine," she said with a shrug. "I don't want to bleed to death or anything, so I'll do it."

"Good."

"But *not* because you told me to."

"Whatever." He pushed away from the counter, turned his back on her and stalked into the bedroom.

He didn't see her stick her tongue out at him. But she enjoyed doing it anyway.

Wincing, Abby awkwardly shifted on the granite counter and dragged her injured foot out of the sink and onto her lap.

"Are you moving?" he called from the other room.

"Yes, master, I'm doing the tango," she snapped angrily.

"Well, sit the hell down."

She heard him throwing broken glass into a trashcan and flinched at every crash and tinkle of what had been a really lovely lamp. Her own fault. She'd obviously made enough noise that he'd heard her at the door. Some spy she'd make.

Pulling the towel away from her foot, she looked at the slice in her skin and flinched.

"Put it back," he ordered from the other room and she stared at the open doorway.

"How did you know it was off?"

"I know *you*."

"I used to be able to say the same about you, you know," she called back, as she once again tucked her now-ruined, bloody designer hand towel to her injured foot.

"Abby…"

"Who is she?"

Another crash of glass hitting the trash can, then silence.

"Luke?"

He appeared in the open doorway. Bare-chested, he wore a pair of old jeans that were worn and faded and fit him like a second skin. The denim hung low on his hips and the top two buttons were undone. The hem of his jeans stacked up atop his bare feet and Abby had to swallow hard against a sharp jolt of lust and hunger that she really didn't want to be feeling at the moment.

She had to force herself to remember what she'd overheard. He'd told Katherine that he was going to stay here, with Abby, until he had what he was after. And though she didn't know exactly what that meant, it didn't fill her with giddy joy.

"Katherine," she repeated. "Who is she? Do I know her?"

"No," he said on a sigh, "you don't know her."

Inside her, something broke. Shattered, just as completely as that antique lamp.

She'd suspected another woman.

But, oh God, how she'd been hoping she was wrong.

"It's not what you think."

Abby laughed and it sounded brittle, even to her. "I wonder how many husbands have said that to how many trusting wives."

He came into the room and lifted her foot off her lap.

"Don't. I don't want you to help me. I don't want—"

"I don't give a good damn what you want, Abby."

"Oh, I think that's perfectly obvious, but thanks

for saying it out loud." She sniffed and hated herself for it. While he inspected her injury, she wiped away a few stray tears with the backs of her hands.

"You don't understand."

"Then explain it to me."

"I can't."

"You won't. There's a difference."

"You should have stitches."

"No. No doctors. No hospitals."

He glanced at her, and probably saw both the fear and pain in her eyes. Because he slowly nodded and said, "Okay. We'll take care of it here."

Abby blew out a shuddering breath. "Okay."

"Good thing you always keep a first-aid kit in all the bathrooms."

"Yeah, that's me. Born under a lucky star."

His jaw worked, but he didn't say anything as he reached into a cupboard, pulled out the white box marked with a big red cross and opened it.

"Why were you listening at the door?" he asked as he situated a couple of butterfly bandages over the cut on her foot.

"Why do you think?" She answered his question with a question and knew this conversation wouldn't go anywhere.

"Because you don't trust me."

"Bingo. And it seems I have good reason."

"Things aren't always what they seem, Abby." When he was satisfied with the butterflies, he took a roll of gauze and carefully wrapped several layers around her foot, then cut some adhesive tape to hold it in place.

But he didn't let her go. Instead, he cradled her foot in the palm of his hand and slowly, gently, stroked her skin.

"Luke, I don't want you—"

"Now who's the liar?" he asked, his voice a low rumble of sound that seemed to reverberate inside her.

Her heart ached, making it nearly impossible to draw a breath. She looked into his eyes and saw the man she'd fallen in love with so long ago. She felt his touch and still fired to it. But it wasn't that easy anymore. No matter how much she wanted him…he simply wasn't the man she had thought she knew.

"I just heard you on the phone with another woman," she reminded him. "Is it really so easy for you to move from me to her and back again?"

A muscle in his jaw twitched and his eyes narrowed. "I've already given you my word that I've never cheated on you, Abby."

"Yes, but what's your word worth these days, Luke?"

He took a breath and released it slowly, keeping his gaze fixed on hers. Gently setting her injured foot back in her lap, he picked up her hands and smoothed his thumbs across her skin. "I know I'm asking a lot here. I know you think you have reason to doubt me—"

"I *think?*"

"But," he interrupted sharply, "I'm asking you to try to trust me. To reach back, to look at all of our years together and try to find that trust again." He dropped her hands, lifted his and cupped her face in his palms. "Please, Abby. Just try to trust me for a little while. Can you do that?"

She covered his hands with hers and though she felt the warmth of him, it didn't dispel the chill inside her. "I don't know."

He closed his eyes as if against a wound so deep he couldn't bear it. And when he looked at her again, there was grim resolve in his dark eyes. "Try Abby," he said softly. "Just promise me you'll try."

The following morning, Abby's foot throbbed and her head felt as though it was stuffed with cotton. She hadn't gotten any sleep and a quick look in her mirror told her that those sleepless hours had been etched onto her face.

Her eyes felt gritty and her stomach seemed to be in a perpetual spin and lurch. She couldn't forget Luke's gentleness with her and yet, the memory of him talking to another woman was just as clear. She felt as if she was a Ping-Pong ball, slamming back and forth between players bent on smashing her.

"Ms. Talbot?"

Abby jerked at the intrusion and looked up to find her assistant standing in the open doorway of her office. God, she was so unfocused she hadn't even heard the door open.

"What is it, Donna?"

"Phone call for you on line two. Our French

office. I tried buzzing you," Donna said, barely concealing her impatience. "You didn't respond."

"Sorry," Abby shook her head, tried to get her mind back on business. "Who's on the line?"

Donna rolled her eyes. "I just told you that. The French office. You were supposed to call them first thing this morning."

Abby sighed, rubbed at a spot between her eyes and murmured, "I guess I forgot."

"Mr. Wainwright isn't happy about this," Donna said, and the fiftyish woman looked as snippy as an old maid librarian shushing constant whisperers.

"Thank you," Abby said, and bit her lip to keep from firing the woman. After all, it was Abby's own fault the work wasn't getting done.

Donna checked a memo pad she held in one hand. "When you've dealt with Michel, you have a twelve-thirty lunch with marketing and then a two o'clock with the buyer from London."

"Fine," Abby muttered, already reaching for the phone.

"And, you should know," Donna added before she could pick up the receiver, "Mr. Wainwright wants to see you in his office before you leave today."

Perfect.

Abby's head pounded and her throat tightened. Stress, she thought. Too much stress. Her mother's murder. The attempt on her own life. Luke's lying. A divorce. Her foot hurt, her stomach was churning and her eyes felt like two marbles in a bucket of damp sand.

There was just too much.

Too much to think about.

Too much to worry about.

And now she had to soothe Michel Andre's feelings because she'd forgotten to call him. Then the lunch meeting. Then Mr. Wainwright.

Her fingers tapped idly on the receiver, but she didn't pick it up. She glanced at the blinking white hold light on the phone and knew she should pick up the darn phone.

But she just couldn't make herself do it.

"Ms. Talbot?" Donna prompted. "Line two?"

Abby hardly heard her over the roaring in her own ears. She couldn't do this anymore. Couldn't pretend that this job, the perfume industry, mattered to her in the slightest. It wasn't as if she needed the income. It wasn't as if she *had* to be doing a job she no longer cared about.

So why was she here?

She couldn't come up with a single reason.

"That's it," she said, grabbing her purse from the bottom right desk drawer and then standing up. She looked at Donna's surprised expression and nearly laughed. Shrugging into her suit jacket, she said, "Tell Mr. Wainwright I won't be able to come to his office today."

"He won't be happy."

"Curiously enough," Abby said as she walked to the door, forcing Donna to step aside to make room, "that's not my problem anymore. I quit."

Eight

That afternoon, Katherine Shaker checked her ear mic and then pulled her short brown hair over her ears to cover it. "I'm set," she said, picking up her purse and flipping it open to make sure her nine millimeter was tucked inside. It was.

"Fine," Luke said, slipping his own gun behind his back, under the waistband of his jeans. Pulling his sweatshirt down to cover the bulge, he grabbed his keys from his pocket and jingled them in the palm of his hand. "Keep the tail on Abby. Don't let her out of your sight."

"I've been on her ass for the past two days, remember?" Katherine smirked at him. "I've been doing this a long time, Talbot. I really don't need you to tell me how to do my job."

"Yeah?" Luke asked, glancing around the crowded central office to make sure no other agents were close enough to overhear. "If you're so damn good at your job, you'd know enough not to call me at home."

She had the grace to flush a little, but immediately stiffened her spine and lifted her chin. "An error I regret."

"No more than I do," he countered, remembering finding Abby at his bedroom door, eavesdropping on his conversation with Katherine.

He could recall with utmost clarity the look of wounded betrayal in her eyes and he wanted to kick his own ass. But what could he have done differently? It wasn't as though he could tell her that he had been talking to a fellow agent about Abby's safety.

Tom had assigned Katherine Shaker to help Luke out, knowing that the woman's elegant look and manner would fit in well around the country club and Eastwick society. She had a good cover story—the estranged wife of a wealthy older man, shopping for a new home. That way, she could move among the locals, frequent the country club and be able to keep tabs on Abby without her getting suspicious.

Or, more suspicious than she already was.

"Look, Abby's walking a fine line right now," Luke said, inwardly cringing at the understatement. He hated admitting, even to himself, that *he* himself had added to Abby's worries. "She knows her mother was murdered—probably by one of the people she considers a friend. She damn near died herself, and she can't trust her husband anymore."

For the first time since he'd known her, Luke saw sympathy flash in Katherine's eyes for a split second. "It's hard, I know," she said, swinging her purse strap over her shoulder. "Hell, Luke. Marriage is tough enough under normal circumstances. And God knows nothing about our job is *normal*."

"True," he acknowledged and wondered again if he shouldn't just tell Abby the truth and damn the consequences.

"Telling her wouldn't be a good idea," Katherine said, as if she were reading his mind.

He laughed shortly, ruefully. "What're you, psychic?"

"No," Katherine said wryly, "it's just that you're not the first agent to consider telling their spouse the truth about what they do."

The normal, everyday office noise faded into the background. It was as if all the keyboards had been silenced and all the other agents had left the room. Katherine's pretty features were blank, revealing nothing and yet, Luke had known her for a few years. He knew she had once been engaged to a medical doctor, but that the relationship had ended. Badly.

"Did you?" he asked quietly.

She shifted a look first right, then left, then back to him. "Yeah. If you ever repeat this, I'll deny it, call you a liar and maybe even put out a contract on you," she warned with only a slight smile on her face. "But yes. I told my fiancé the truth. I know it was against regs, but I felt like he deserved to know who he was marrying. What I did for a living."

"And…?"

"And," she repeated, "you know who my husband is. You know he works for this agency. And you know he's not a doctor."

"He didn't take it well." Luke eased down to perch on the edge of his desk.

"You could say that," Katherine admitted with a half shrug. "You could also say I saw sparks from the soles of his feet as he ran away from me at top speed."

"I'm sorry."

She shrugged again. "So was I. At the time. You know, David wasn't a bad guy. He just wasn't prepared to hear that the woman he thought he loved was a spy, not a computer software analyst." Inhaling sharply, she straightened up and said, "So, enough of memory lane. I've got to get moving if you want me to start the tail on your wife this afternoon."

"Right. And thanks, Kat."

"Later."

The tall, self possessed woman walked across the busy room, head held high, but Luke wasn't fooled. He had heard the old sadness in his friend's voice and knew the betrayal by her fiancé still hurt her. He appreciated the fact that she'd told him any of this at all—she'd taken a chance. If their supervisors ever found out she'd talked about the agency to a civilian, her career would be over. But at the same time, he wondered if Abby would react the same way? Would she be appalled? Or relieved?

He would probably never know.

"Thanks for coming," Mary said when she opened her front door to Abby an hour later. "Kane really wants you to hear the tape."

"I can't believe he's still got it," Abby said, tossing her purse down onto the hall table in her friend's elegant foyer. Favoring her injured foot, Abby fought the urge to kick off her designer mules. She'd worn them that morning to avoid having to wear closed shoes over the bandages. But after several hours, the throbbing was starting to reverberate throughout her body and all she really wanted to do was go home and prop up her foot.

"Oh, Kane's too thorough to ever throw something like that away. The police have a copy, but he kept the original. I don't think they know that, but…" Mary shrugged and tucked her hair behind her ear.

Abby glanced around the house as she followed her friend down the hall and then up the stairs to Kane's office. Paintings, done by Mary herself, dotted the walls, bright splashes of vivid color. The house itself was quiet and cool, and Abby appreciated the peace.

Ever since she'd walked out on her job, her brain had been clamoring with silent shrieks, all demanding that she explain herself. But she couldn't. All she knew for sure was that leaving that office, she'd taken her first easy breath in weeks. It was as if she'd escaped prison. Where she would go from here, she had no idea. But that first step had officially been taken and, despite the rational voice in her mind trying to guilt her into going back, she was confident with her decision.

Trying to refocus her mind, Abby asked, "This is the call Kane received from some woman accusing you of killing my mother?"

"Yes." Mary paused on the stairs, turned back and looked at Abby. "I can't tell you how much it means to me, knowing that you believe I would never have hurt Bunny. Even as furious as she could make me," Mary acknowledged, "I would never have hurt her."

Instinctively, Abby reached out, took one of Mary's hands in hers and gave it a squeeze. "Honey, I know that." Then, forcing a smile and a chuckle she didn't really feel, she added, "Besides, Mom could make *anybody* nuts. Including me."

Mary's eyes filled, but she blinked the tears back and smiled in return. "Thanks. Really. Thanks."

"You bet." Abby let her go and continued up the stairs when Mary started walking again. She and Mary had known each other forever. When they were kids, Mary had had a wild, bohemian streak that had made her lively and fun to be around. And though she was quieter now, more centered, there was simply no way that a woman as inherently sweet and gentle as

Mary could murder *anyone*. Least of all, the mother of one of her best friends.

At the landing, Mary turned right and led the way into a room that had been outfitted as a top-of-the-line office space. Filing cabinets, a sleek computer and a fax machine-copier lined the walls and a sofa and comfortable armchair completed the furnishings. There were paintings on the walls and two or three framed photographs of a smiling Kane and Mary together standing on the wide, mahogany desktop.

Kane stood, smiled and held out one hand to Abby. His blue eyes were sharp and he looked casually elegant in black slacks and a white dress shirt, open at the collar. When he spoke, his British accent flavored every word. "Abby. Thank you for coming."

"Of course. Anything I can do." She smiled at Mary, then shifted her gaze back to Kane. "I want to find out who murdered my mother. I *have* to find out. But I want to make it clear, I know that person wasn't Mary."

Kane smiled and draped one arm around Mary's shoulders. When she leaned into him and laid one hand on his chest in a comfortingly familiar gesture, Abby's heart twisted in envy. There was a time she and Luke had been that close. That comfortable together. How she missed it.

"Well then, shall we play the tape so you can try to identify the caller?"

"Yes," Abby said and moved to the desk, Mary standing beside her, gripping her hand for support.

The minute Kane hit the play button, a strange,

distorted voice filled the room. Her words were clear, as the woman implicated Mary in Bunny's death. But her voice was muddy. Indistinct. In fact, if Kane hadn't identified her as a woman, Abby would have been hard-pressed to guess whether it was a male or female voice.

Still, the venom in the caller's tone came through loud and clear. Mary's fingers tightened on Abby's cold hand and stayed like that until the tape was finished and Kane turned the machine off.

"Any ideas?" he asked, watching Abby intently.

"None," she admitted sadly. "Though I feel like I want to burn that tape and cleanse the house with burning sage and cinnamon candles."

"Yeah, that voice gives me the heebies, too," Mary said softly, staring at the machine as if half expecting the caller to step right out of the recorder and threaten them all in person.

"Who would do that?" Abby whispered.

"Someone trying to keep suspicion off herself."

"You're sure it's a woman talking? Kind of hard to tell, isn't it?"

"The expert I took the tape to insists that the cadence of speech and some of the colloquialisms definitely point the way to female."

"I'll take your word for it," Abby said with a shudder. "I'm just glad this tape didn't incriminate Mary."

"Not a chance," Kane said and reached for the woman he loved, pulling her into a close embrace and kissing the top of her head for good measure.

Envy pricked at her again and Abby told herself she should be ashamed of the feeling. Mary deserved her happiness with Kane. Just because Abby herself was miserable, didn't mean she wanted to see all of her friends in the same boat.

"I'm sorry you didn't recognize the caller," Kane said, disappointment clear in his tone. "But thank you for trying."

Abby nodded. "The police say they still have no leads in my mother's death."

"Was the killer really that clever, you think?"

"Clever enough to escape detection so far," Abby said.

"No crime is perfect," Kane told them both. "After all, if criminals were smart, the prisons wouldn't be so crowded, now would they?"

Abby smiled in spite of her day from hell. "Good point." She checked her wristwatch and sighed. "I'm sorry, but I should run."

"Oh," Mary said, "stay and have some coffee." She paused and added in a coaxing voice, "I have cake…."

"Chocolate?" Abby asked.

"Is there another kind?" Mary teased.

"Sold," Abby said. "Coffee and chocolate. Sounds like just what I need after the day I've had."

"Bad?"

"Doesn't begin to describe it," Abby assured her.

"I'm all ears." Then she turned to Kane. "Would you like to join us?"

Kane, a wise man, shook his head and sat down

at his desk. "No, thank you, love. I'll leave you to it and get some of my own work done."

Mary bent down for a quick kiss, then straightened, and smiled at Abby. "Okay, let's go gorge on chocolate while you tell me what's wrong."

"Deal," Abby said, heading out of the room.

"Hey," Mary asked, following behind her, "why are you limping?"

Frustrated, and stuffed with chocolate and coffee, Abby headed home an hour later.

"So," she said, with a quick glance at her own reflection in the rearview mirror. "A bumper day for you. Hell, a record week. Murder attempt. Philandering husband. And now, unemployed."

Her hands tightened on the steering wheel of her sleek, two-seater sports car. When the signal turned from green to yellow, she slowed down, preparing to stop. Classic rock poured from the sound system and the dashboard clock read four forty-five.

The sky was dark and heavy with rain clouds. The wind rushed past her car, picked up dry leaves and twirled them off down the street. A kid on a bicycle popped a wheelie, tumbled off the back end of the bike and cracked his helmeted head on the sidewalk.

"Ouch," Abby muttered, then relieved, watched the kid bound up, jump onto his bike and wheel off down the sidewalk. As she turned her head to the front, she caught a glimpse of a blue car behind her.

For a second or two, she didn't think anything of

it. Then a niggling thought gnawed at the edges of her mind. Over the past couple of days, she'd seen that blue car behind her half a dozen times or more. It was never very close, usually keeping at least one car between them, but it was *there*.

Just like now.

Without turning her head, she glanced again into the mirror and tried to notice everything without actually staring. A woman sat at the wheel. Vaguely familiar and yet, a stranger. Brown hair, dark glasses, despite the lowering gloom of the day and a nondescript, late-model blue compact.

Idly tapping her fingers to the beat of the music, Abby kept tossing glances at the woman behind her, trying to place her. Trying to remember where she'd seen her and when. But it just wasn't coming.

Still, it creeped her out enough that her insides were jumping and her heart rate accelerated. *Someone* had tried to kill her. *Someone* had poisoned her champagne. Maybe this was the person. Maybe she'd tired of being sneaky and had decided to just run Abby off the road somehow. Make her death look like a tragic traffic accident.

Mouth suddenly dry, Abby reached out and punched the radio off button. Silence dropped onto her like a suffocating blanket. Rummaging one-handed into her purse, Abby blindly found her cell phone, flipped it open and hit speed dial for Luke.

"Overreacting much?" she asked herself, trying to find humor in the situation and missing com-

pletely. This wasn't funny. And it wasn't her imagination. She'd seen that car before. Seconds ticked
past as she listened to Luke's phone ring. And ring.
And ring. No answer.

One hand fisted on the steering wheel, Abby
glanced from the woman behind her to the traffic
light in front of her, anxiously awaiting her turn to
get moving. Meanwhile, Luke's voice mail kicked in.
Abby hung up, then dialed again, never taking her
free hand off the steering wheel.

When the light turned green, Abby punched the
gas pedal to the floor and held on while her car's
powerful engine jumped to life. Instantly, the tiny
sports car leaped off the line like a cheetah going
from zero to sixty in a blink.

She tore down the road and noted that the blue car
behind her kept pace. Always leaving room between
them, the car nonetheless stayed right with her. Abby
could hardly draw breath. Her lungs felt as though
they were in a vise and her heartbeat thundered in her
chest, pounding against her rib cage as if it was trying
to escape its prison and fly free.

"Abby?" Luke's voice came, warm and familiar
in her ear.

God, he sounded good.

"Luke, somebody's behind me. I mean following
me. In a blue car." She took a right turn, barely
braking and felt her tires skid slightly, then find
purchase again. Trees were whizzing past as she
headed for the interstate on-ramp. She wasn't going

to keep driving at high speeds on city streets where she could run down a kid chasing a ball into the street.

"What?" he asked. "Following you?"

"Yes," she screamed in a sudden burst of fury at men who don't listen. "Aren't you listening to me? A blue car. A woman driving. I've seen her a lot the past few days. Just didn't notice till now."

"Ah, God. Abby…" His voice dropped a notch.

Abby steered around a slow-moving minivan and blew into the fast lane, wishing she were closer to the damn interstate. Eastwick had never seemed so big before. The blue car was closer now. She flew through a red light and the honking horns that blasted in her wake made her cringe and say a silent prayer.

"It's not stopping," she said through gritted teeth. "What do I do? Where do I go?"

"Abby, listen. You don't have to be scared," Luke was saying, his voice urgent now.

She laughed hysterically, heard the sound and took a gulp of breath to steady herself. "How can I help being *scared?*" she shouted frantically. "Somebody's trying to kill me again!"

"No, babe," he said, "it's okay. The driver of the blue car is a friend of mine."

"What?" She threw another glance in the rear-view mirror, her foot easing off the gas pedal incrementally. Did the blue car slow down, too?

"A friend, Abby. The driver is just keeping an eye on you. To keep you safe."

"Safe?" She eased up further on the gas. Fury was quickly replacing the stark terror she'd known only a moment or two ago. How could he do this to her? How could he terrify her like this? He knew she was already on an emotional cliff ready to topple. "I'm driving like a maniac, running red lights and speeding through town trying to get away from your *friend?*"

"I can explain."

"No, you son of a bitch," Abby shrieked, gripping the phone so tight, she was surprised Luke wasn't choking in response, "you *can't.* You scared me. You set up a stranger to follow me. You should have *told* me!"

She took her foot off the gas completely and kept her gaze on the rearview mirror as the blue car came closer…fast. Narrowing her eyes, she tried to see the driver, but the sun's glare on the windshield made that impossible.

Fear came back in a rush.

"Luke…"

"What's wrong?" he said, picking up on the worry in her voice.

"The car…" she said in short bursts, filled with exploding terror. "Oh…my…God…it's…not…slowing…down…"

He shouted into her ear. "What do you mean?"

"Oh God!" Abby dropped the phone, grabbed hold of the steering wheel and screamed as the blue car rammed her squarely. Her little car screeched sideways across the pavement. Eyes wild, heart pounding, she watched, helpless as she careened toward a light pole with no way to stop.

The last thing she heard was Luke's voice screaming her name.

Nine

Luke couldn't breathe.

With the sound of Abby's scream still ringing in his ears, he drove like a crazy man, following the GPS signal he was picking up from her car. From a distance, he saw an ambulance, a couple of fire trucks and three police cruisers parked in a semicircle around the scene of an accident.

As he slammed on the brakes, he noted a spiral of smoke dancing and twisting in the air as it lifted from the crushed hood of a car.

Abby's car.

"Ah, God, no…"

He threw his car into Park, turned off the engine then bolted into the gathering crowd. Only half listening to the whispered shock in the voices of the people straining to see, he pushed through them all, straight-arming his way to the front of the crowd.

He couldn't remember ever knowing this kind of bone-deep terror. It was as if his whole body was wrapped in ice that was slowly squeezing the life out of him. Abby's face floated in the forefront of his mind and was the only thing that kept him moving when he thought he couldn't take another step. Luke fought the fear jangling inside, as he'd been taught to do. But he knew, deep in his core, that if Abby were hurt bad— or worse—nothing in his life would be worth a damn.

"Stop it! I'm telling you, I'm fine, so quit trying to poke and prod at me!"

Abby's voice lifted over the muttering crowd and sounded so angry, so full of life and temper, relief plowed into Luke with the force of a freight train. His step faltered as he closed his eyes, grinned and took his first easy breath in way too long. His heartbeat kicked into life again as he heard her, clearly furious, tear a strip off somebody. He'd never heard anything more beautiful in his life.

"Somebody get me a phone," she demanded in her best Queen to Peasant tone. "Or find *my* phone. It's in my car—or what's left of my car."

"We'll get you a phone later," a deep voice said.

"Now," Abby responded and Luke wished the guy arguing with his wife luck. Because when Abby used that tone in her voice, heads were about to roll. God, he loved that woman.

"Lady, if you don't let me check your eyes for signs of concussion…" the EMT spoke quietly, with a sort of forced patience.

"I'll show you a concussion," Abby shouted and Luke pushed to the front of the crowd in time to see her give the poor man trying to help her a vicious shove.

"Ma'am?" A young patrol cop approached her hesitantly and Luke couldn't blame him for his caution. "If you'll just tell us exactly what happened…"

Luke watched as his delicate, beautiful wife ripped the blood pressure cuff off her upper arm and threw it at the EMT before turning on the cop, who looked as though he would rather be *anywhere* else.

"I've *told* you already," Abby snarled. "Pole. Car." Her palms smacked together. "Car hit pole." She threw her hands wide. "How hard is that to understand? Now, listen carefully. I. Need. A. Phone."

"Geez, lady…" The young cop backed up a step.

"Abby!" Luke called her name and she spun around fast. She had a small cut above her eye, but other than that, didn't seem to have a mark on her and for that, Luke thought, he would be forever in debt to whoever had kept her safe.

Her gaze caught his and relief, followed quickly by fury, flashed across her eyes.

"Luke!" She took a step toward him, then stopped and looked at the cop. "I don't need the phone now, after all. This is my husband."

The cop gave him a sympathetic glance, then backed off.

"Abby," Luke said again, stalking across the few feet separating them. Damn it, call him crazy, but he *loved* seeing that furious glint in her eyes. Even if it was directed at him. He'd been so scared. So terrified that he'd lost her. Never again get to hold her, kiss her, tell her that he loved her.

Then he got close, Abby muttered, "You son of a bitch!" and slapped him hard.

He felt as though his eyeballs were jittering with the force of the blow but before he could respond, she leaped at him, wrapping her arms around his neck and holding on as if it meant her life.

"I'm sorry," she muttered thickly. "I didn't mean to hit you. I'm just—"

"It's okay, baby," he assured her, his tone soothing, his hands moving up and down her back in a caress meant to comfort.

She burrowed even closer, shaking her head, tightening her grip on him. "God, Luke, I was so scared."

"Me, too, baby," he whispered, burying his face in the curve of her neck. He inhaled her scent, kissed the pulse point at the base of her throat and held her until she stopped trembling. "Me, too."

The emergency workers stayed back, giving them as much privacy as being in the center of a crowd could afford. After a long couple of minutes, though, when Luke was pretty sure he could stand letting go of her briefly, he pulled her off him and held her at arm's length. "Are you okay?"

"I'm fine," she said, but her voice had a hitch in it. "I just can't seem to stop shaking."

"Shock," he whispered, smoothing her hair back from her face with a gentle touch. Right now, she was holding it together. He knew that soon, the shock would really settle in and she'd be lucky to stand up under her own power.

"If you want my opinion," the EMT said, as he gathered up his blood pressure cuff and rolled it tightly, "we don't know if she's fine or not, since she wouldn't let us examine her."

She turned and fixed a glare on the guy. "My blood pressure is a little high because somebody ran me off the road!"

"What're you talking about?" Luke demanded, grabbing her arm and turning her back around to face him. "This wasn't an accident?"

"The only accident," Abby told him quietly, "is that I'm still alive." She shoved her hair back and Luke noticed that her eyes looked a little wild. Too much adrenaline in her system.

"I'm talking about your *friend*," Abby snapped, "the one who was following me."

"Impossible," he said thickly, instinctively scanning the area around them for the signs of the blue car Katherine Shaker had been driving. But there was nothing. Not a sign of her.

And wasn't that unusual?

If Katherine had seen Abby's accident, she would have stayed with her until help came. So

why wasn't she there? And if she wasn't there…
where the hell was she?

Abby swayed unsteadily against him and Luke
shut down every thought but his wife's safety.

"Come on. You need to sit down." He walked her
to the curb, one arm around her waist, and eased her
down carefully, as if she were made of the most
fragile porcelain. "You're not okay, Ab…"

"She might have a concussion." The EMT
shrugged and shook his head. "Can't tell because
she won't let me check her out."

"I told you I don't need to be checked," Abby
said, temper sparking again as she lifted her gaze to
Luke's. Those beautiful eyes of hers filled with tears
and the beginnings of pain he knew would soon start
screaming at her. "I just want to go home."

Luke watched her and noted how pale she was,
how glassy her eyes suddenly looked and he worried
about that cut on her forehead. She was walking and
talking now, but adrenaline would keep her moving
for a couple hours. When that wore off and shock set
in, she was going to start feeling aches and pains in
muscles she didn't even know she had.

"Abby," he said, dropping to one knee in front of her,
taking both of her hands in his. "You're going to ride
to the hospital with these guys and get checked out."

"No, I'm not." Scowling first at Luke, then the
EMT and then back again, "I don't need a hospital
and you can't make me go."

One eyebrow lifted. "Wanna bet?"

The police were dispersing the crowd and the fire-fighters were putting their gear away. Nearly sundown, the shadows were long and the temperature was cool and dropping fast. Abby shivered and Luke shrugged out of his old, brown leather bomber jacket and draped it around her shoulders.

"Abby," he said, meeting her gaze and holding it, "you're going to the hospital. Now, you can go under your own steam or I'll tie you to a gurney."

She frowned at him. "You'd do that to me?"

"In a heartbeat."

She studied him for a long minute or two, trying to decide whether or not he meant what he was saying. Finally, she lowered her gaze and muttered, "Fine."

"Good choice," Luke said and helped her to stand again. Walking her to the open doors of the ambulance, he handed her off to the paramedic and said, "I'll follow you."

She stopped. "You're not riding with me?"

He wanted to. Wanted to be right by her side, insuring that nothing else bad would ever happen to her. But there were a couple of things he had to check out. For her sake as well as his own.

"I'll be right behind you."

She nodded stiffly, then glanced past him to where her cute little sports car sat smoking, crumpled around the base of the lamp pole.

Luke followed her gaze and stiffened. The passenger side was crunched completely, shoved so far into the interior of the car that Abby, sitting on the driver's side, had probably felt the cold steel brush her body. Thank God, no one had been with her. Thank God the driver's side was relatively unscathed.

"Thank God for air bags," she muttered, as if reading his mind.

"Amen to that." Luke dropped a kiss on her forehead, then waved at one of the paramedics. "Go on and don't give these guys a hard time. I'll see you at the hospital."

Once she was inside the truck and the doors were closed, he stood back and watched as the ambulance roared off. Then he turned his gaze onto what was left of the curious crowd, searching for a familiar face. When he didn't find it, Luke walked over to the closest cop, flashed his ID badge and asked, "Any witnesses?"

The young cop's eyes bulged with surprise as he looked from the government ID to Luke's hard, cold eyes. "No, sir. There's some evidence that another car was involved like your wife said. Some blue paint on the rear right panel of your wife's car. Otherwise, nothing."

"Fine." Luke left the younger man to fill out his report and walked over to what was left of Abby's car. He checked out the rear panel himself and squatting beside the wreck, he saw the streak of blue imbedded in the scarred metal.

Careful not to touch it, for fear of disturbing evidence, Luke studied that paint as his mind raced. If Katherine had run Abby off the road, then someone had gotten to her. Which he just didn't believe.

Katherine Shaker was not only one of their best agents, she was a friend. Luke had trusted her with his life on more than one occasion.

So, if his fellow agent hadn't been behind this accident, that meant someone else had. And if they were driving Katherine's car, then where was Katherine? And who in Eastwick had been good enough to take out a trained, experienced agent?

He stood up, forced his anger into a tight, hard ball in the pit of his stomach and grabbed for his cell phone. Punching the speed dial, he called Tom Kennedy.

When the other man answered, Luke asked abruptly, "Have you heard from Katherine?"

"No. Nothing in three hours. She missed her last check-in."

"This doesn't look good."

"You think?" Tom's voice was tight and gruff. "How's your wife?"

"Probably fine, considering. She's on her way to the hospital."

"Go join her. We'll find Katherine."

"Keep me posted," Luke said and hung up, shoving his phone into his shirt pocket. Then he forgot about everything else, climbed into his car and followed his heart to Abby.

Every square inch of her body ached.

Abby winced as she pushed herself higher on the pillows at her back, then sighed in relief to be safe in her own house, in her own bed.

With her husband right beside her.

Luke had been great. Okay, he'd bullied her into going to the hospital, but he'd sat with her in the emergency room and held her hand while she was being examined. Then he'd carried her from the car to their bedroom and tenderly undressed her and tucked her into bed.

She closed her eyes and felt his hands on her again.

"Going to sleep?" Luke asked as he came into the room, carrying a tray.

Abby's eyes flew open and she watched him cross the room to stand by her side. "No," she said. "I'm too wired to sleep and too sore to be awake."

"I'm just grateful that you're *only* sore," he said, setting the tray holding a cup of tea and some soup down on the table beside the bed. "You were lucky."

"I know," she said and reached for his hand. Tugging him down onto the edge of the mattress, she looked up into his eyes so she could watch him as she asked him, "Did the police find your 'friend'?"

Those eyes she knew so well shuttered, locking her out and confirming her fears that Luke was still lying to her, keeping her at arm's length, no matter how differently his actions spoke.

"No," he said, then added, "but it wasn't Katherine who hit you."

"Katherine?" she repeated. "The woman I heard you talking to the other night?"

"Yes." He watched her and she knew he must have seen what she was thinking on her face because he

said quickly, "I'm not having an affair with Kath
erine. She's a friend. From work."

Abby let go of his hand and turned her face away
from him. A short, harsh laugh shot from her throat.
"From work? You had a computer analyst following me to keep me safe? Please, Luke. At least lie
convincingly."

The phone rang and Luke reached for it. Abby
didn't want to look at him, but couldn't help herself.
She turned her head on the pillow and watched as her
husband's features tightened and his eyes darkened
until they were almost black.

"I understand," he said. "When?"

Tension spiraled in the room and Abby scooted
up on the pillows again until she was almost sitting
straight up. She hardly felt the aches and pains
simmering in her body. Instead, every sense was
locked on Luke.

She noted the ramrod stiffness of his spine, the
white-knuckled grip he had on the phone and the
grim slash of his mouth as he nodded to whoever was
speaking to him.

"Tomorrow then," Luke said. "Fine." He hung up
with a forced carefulness that told Abby what he really
wanted to do was throw the phone across the room.

"What is it?" she asked, hoping that this time he
wouldn't lie. That this time, she'd be able to see in
his eyes that he was being honest with her.

He turned his head and speared her with a look.
"That was the office."

"The office?" she repeated in disbelief. "A *computer* problem upset you this much?"

He gave a strangled laugh, then reached up and shoved both hands through his hair before scraping his palms across his face. Finally, he looked at her again, with a thoughtful, considering air.

"What?" she demanded, feeling nerves begin to flutter to life in her belly. "What is it? Luke, please just *tell* me. I can take anything but more lies."

"I think you can," he said finally, nodding to himself as if he'd made a decision. Then, speaking slowly, he picked up one of her hands and held it tightly. "I should have told you this a long time ago. But I wasn't allowed. It's against the rules."

"What rules?" Abby didn't understand any of this, but just thinking that someone else had been behind her husband lying to her made her furious. "You mean you've been lying to me because you were forced to?"

"Yeah," he acknowledged, his eyes still dark, his features still tight. "That's about it. In my business, you never tell the truth. Lies keep you alive."

Fear blossomed in her chest and she clung to his hand. "Alive? Luke, I don't—"

He cut her off. "Abby, I'm going to tell you something that I'm not supposed to reveal to anyone."

Her nerves had nerves now. The spinning, churning sensation in her stomach quadrupled and she was suddenly grateful she hadn't eaten recently. Luke's expression was so still, so serious, she was half-terrified to hear what he wanted to tell her.

But she'd had enough of subterfuge.

She wanted answers.

No matter what they were.

"First, it wasn't Katherine who rammed your car," he said.

"How do you know?" she managed to ask and studied his face in the soft glow of lamplight. Because she was watching him so closely, she saw fury glitter in his eyes before it was shut down in the next instant.

"Because she was just found, unconscious in an alley."

Abby sucked in a gulp of air then released it slowly, half-afraid she wouldn't be able to draw another when she needed it. "Is she all right?"

"She will be," Luke said, and tightened his grip on her hand. "Whoever bashed her over the head used her car to run you off the road. The car hasn't been found yet, but when it is, we're hoping there'll be some evidence to point to whoever did this."

Abby shook her head as she stared at him. "None of this makes sense, Luke."

"It does if you have the missing piece of the puzzle," he said tightly.

"Which is…?"

He blew out a breath. "Katherine's not a computer analyst, Abby. Neither am I."

This, she hadn't expected. Cheating on her, yes. Lying to her definitely. But why would a man lie about his *job?* She swallowed hard and braced herself. "What exactly are you saying?"

He locked his gaze with hers and said simply, "I'm a spy."

Ten

Luke watched her, waiting for her reaction.

When it came, it wasn't what he'd been expecting.

Her laughter spilled from her in long, breathless explosions of sound. Pushing free of his grasp, she flopped back against the pillows, closed her eyes, gasped for breath and laughed even harder.

"Oh, that's wonderful," she finally said, tears streaming down her cheeks. She lifted one hand and shook her head. "Oh God, a *spy?*"

Luke stood up and glared down at her. "What the hell is so damn funny?"

"Please…" A few more giggles escaped before she was able to control herself again. When she did, she wiped away her tears, blew out a breath and looked up at him. "Of all the silly, stupid stories to come up with. Honestly, Luke, if you're going to continue lying to me, at least make them *believable* lies."

"I'm not lying."

"Right," Abby said, still half smiling, "and as soon as Prince Charles arranges for a divorce, I'll be leaving you and setting up house in Windsor Castle."

"Funny."

"No funnier than your story."

Here was irony for you, he thought grimly. He finally spilled his guts, broke his oath to the agency and she thought it was just one more lie.

"Do you mean now that I'm actually telling you the truth, you don't believe me?"

"Truth?" Blue eyes narrowed, her laughter fading, smile slipping away, she pushed herself up and stared at him as though she'd never seen him before. "You're telling me that you, my husband the computer software analyst, are really James Bond?"

Luke shoved both hands into his jeans pockets and fisted those hands in helpless frustration. "Just so you know? We *hate* those movies."

"Oh do *we?*" She snorted. "Can't imagine why. All those wonderful toys."

She threw the blankets off and stood facing him. Luke noted the high color on her cheeks, the flash of temper sparking in her eyes and knew that this wasn't going to be easy, truth or not. Her blond hair hung loose around her shoulders and her breasts beneath her dark green, silk nightgown heaved with every breath.

"James Bond is fiction. What I do is *real*. Abby, I took an oath to never tell anyone what I do for a living. And until tonight, I never had."

"An oath."

"That's right."

"And you're a spy."

"I prefer the term undercover operative."

"Oh, sure," she nodded, those sparks in her eyes glittering hotly, "wouldn't want to use the wrong term."

He took her upper arm in a firm grip, but she yanked herself free and backed up a step or two. "Don't. Just don't even touch me right now," she warned. Her steps hesitant at first, then fed by the temper churning within, she stomped around the perimeter of the master bedroom.

Her bare feet were soundless on the thick carpet, but her breath huffed in and out of her body in impatient bursts. "Why would you tell me something like this?" she demanded, never stopping long enough for him to get a hold of her again.

"Because I'm tired of lying to you," Luke said, standing still, letting only his gaze follow her erratic movements.

She glared at him.

"I'm not going to lose you because you think I'm having a damned affair."

"So you're not having an affair, you're just a spy."

"Right."

She stopped, folded her arms across her chest and tapped one foot against the carpet. "Who's Katherine?"

Hell, he'd already told her this much. Might as well go for the whole story. "Another operative. I've known her for years."

One blond eyebrow lifted.

Luke sighed. "She's married to an upper-level agent. They have three kids."

Abby's features relaxed a little as she tipped her head to one side. "So Katherine the spy is also a mother?"

"Yes."

"And you're not having an affair with her?"

"No."

"Who are you having an affair with?"

He smiled at her. "No one. My wife is an amazing woman—and she's the jealous type."

"No I'm not," she argued, but there was no heat in it.

"You don't have reason to be," Luke assured her, walking carefully across the room. He advanced on her warily, like a man forced to approach a hungry lion.

"I'd like to believe you," she said softly and Luke felt an infinitesimally small flicker of hope spark to life inside him.

"I'm not lying, Abby," he said and reached for the bomber jacket he'd tossed across the foot of the bed. Reaching into the inside pocket, he pulled out a worn leather wallet and handed it to her.

She took it, opened it and stared silently for several long seconds. When she finally lifted her eyes to his, she said, "It's true? You work for the government?"

"It's true."

"Not a software analyst."

"Wouldn't know how to analyze it."

Shaking her head, she looked down at his official ID again and smoothed her fingertips across the photograph of him. "This is surreal."

"I know how it sounds, but it's all true." He took another step toward her. "When we met on the plane to France?"

She looked up at him.

"I was going to Paris to interrogate a suspected terrorist."

"Oh, my…"

"Those phone calls for Lucy you've intercepted? They're from the office. A signal to get me to call in or report in."

"Passwords?"

"In a way." God, how was she taking this? So hard to tell. Hard to know if he'd done the right thing. Hard to know if he'd only made things worse.

Tom Kennedy wouldn't be happy when he heard about this, but damn it, Luke wasn't willing to lose the most important person in his life because of a promise made before he'd even known her. He *wouldn't* lose Abby. Not without a fight.

"Oh, boy," she whispered and, clutching the ID wallet, she walked to the end of the bed and sat. After a moment or two, she asked, "Your last business trip. Why weren't you at the hotel when I called? Were you even in Sacramento?"

"Yes," he said, taking a seat beside her. "I was. I wasn't in the hotel, though. I stayed at a safe house there while investigating the sale of top secret government files to a foreign power."

"Safe house."

"It was an oversight—the hotel not putting you through to a room where the call would have been transferred to me."

"Top secret."

"Abby?"

She blew out a breath and looked down at his ID, still in her hand. "Government files. Foreign powers. Spies. Terrorists."

"You okay?"

"I don't know," she admitted, lifting her head to stare at the man she'd thought she knew so well. Now, everything she had accepted for years was tumbling down around her like a house of cards in a hard wind. "Luke, I just don't know what to think."

"I know it's a lot to take in."

"It really is," she said, handing him his ID and looking deeply into his dark eyes.

"I never wanted to hide this from you, Abby," he said, lifting one hand to cup her cheek. His thumb smoothed over her skin gently. "But I didn't want to risk endangering you by telling you what I do."

"I understand," she said and she really did. It still hurt that he'd kept so much of his life separate from her, but she could at least appreciate why he'd done it.

The room was quiet. Drapes drawn, only the lamplight kept the darkness at bay. She felt her heartbeat tick off the passing seconds and knew she should say something. But darned if she could think of anything.

"By keeping you out of that part of my life, I was supposed to be keeping you safe," Luke said, and reached out to smooth one hand through her hair. "Now, though, I'm wondering if just being married to me isn't enough to put you in danger."

He gaze snapped to his as she instantly understood what he was talking about. "You mean the cyanide? You think that someone who knows who you really are tried to poison me?"

He scowled thoughtfully. "It's a possibility I have to consider." His hand stilled at the back of her neck. "But it doesn't seem likely."

"No," Abby agreed, her mind now beginning to click along at top speed. "It doesn't. No one in Eastwick suspects who you are and it wouldn't make sense for an enemy agent to expose himself or herself," she allowed, "by trying to poison a civilian at a charity dinner." She stopped, blew out a breath. "Wow. I can't believe I actually used a sentence with the words *enemy agent* in it."

He smiled and gave her neck a little squeeze. "Takes a little getting used to, huh?"

Abby turned to look right at him. His features were so familiar. His eyes the same, dark chocolate color she'd always known. His smile still curved one side of his mouth slightly higher than the other. He was the same man she'd always known. And yet...

now that she knew his secret, she imagined she was noticing new things, too.

The sharpness in his eyes. The hard planes of his jaw and the strength that helped him work behind the scenes, undercover, in danger, to serve his country.

And just like that, a swirl of something hot and delicious and overwhelming swept through her. Every bone in her body ached from the accident earlier, but the fresh desire bubbling in her veins was more compelling.

Leaning in toward him, Abby scooted close and clambered into his lap.

"Hey…" His arms came around her middle and held her in place while at the same time, he was looking at her in question. "You're supposed to be resting."

"Don't want to rest," she whispered and brushed her mouth over his, pausing only long enough to tug at his bottom lip with her teeth.

He groaned. "Abby…"

She wiggled her bottom against him and he went hard and ready in an instant.

"Mmm…" Clearly enjoying herself, she squirmed against him again, her bare heat sliding across the fly of his jeans.

His hands slid up and down her back, then dipped beneath the hem of her nightgown and smoothed along her spine, his fingertips dancing gently over her skin. "This is probably not a good idea," he managed to grumble. "You've got to be in some pain and—"

"No," she said, with a soft shake of her head that

sent her hair dancing around her shoulders. "I'm not. Not now."

She kissed him again, this time putting everything she had into it. His lips parted for her and her tongue tangled with his. She felt his heartbeat accelerate, pounding against hers as he held her so tight, she thought her ribs might crack. But she didn't care.

Yes, she had some aches and pains. But her hunger for her husband outstripped every other sensation. She wanted him so badly, she could hardly breathe. This man. The man she'd loved for so long.

When he finally pulled his head back, breaking the kiss that had left them both breathless, he stared into her eyes and whispered, "From the moment I saw you on that plane—" he shook his head and gave her a half smile "—you were all I wanted. All I'll ever want."

She didn't say anything to that, only reached down and quickly undid the buttons on his jeans. He kept a tight grip at her waist and held his breath while she worked. When she freed him, she ran her fingers up and down his thick, rigid length and watched his eyes roll back in his head.

Then she rubbed her thumb over the sensitive tip of him and when his eyes fixed on her again, she confessed, "When that car hit me, when I was sliding into that pole and knew that I could die in an instant, all I could think was…*I'll never touch him again. Never kiss him again.*"

He laid his forehead against hers and whispered her name in a broken sigh.

Her hand tightened on his length and she slowly went up on her knees. Looking down at him, she said softly, "Luke, I thought I was going to die. And I couldn't bear the thought of never being with you again. I need you. I need to feel you inside me."

"I need that, too, baby," he said and held his breath as she lowered herself onto his length. Inch by inch, she took him within her heat, surrounded him in a tight, damp sheath that filled them both with a glory they'd never found anywhere else.

In the lamplit darkness, they moved together, gazes locked, bodies joined, and together, they chased the elusive explosion that would consume them. Time stood still and all that existed was that room and the heat blossoming between them.

And finally, when she threw her head back, screamed his name and clung to his shoulders, Luke groaned, and emptied himself inside her. Then tightening his grip on her, he fell back on the bed and held his world close.

An hour or two later, Abby listened to the steady beat of Luke's heart beneath her ear as she cuddled in close to him. He was sleeping, one arm draped around her shoulder, holding her to his side.

But Abby hadn't been able to close her eyes. She kept seeing that lamppost headed toward her. Kept imagining Luke in dark alleys with guns pointed at him. Every old espionage movie she had ever seen came rushing back in the darkness to taunt her. Haunt her. Terrorize her with thoughts of the kinds of things that Luke faced every time he left their home to go to work.

And she'd never once guessed.

In all the time she'd known him, she had never suspected that he had had such a secret. Which told her exactly how good he was at his job. He was a man who had learned how to compartmentalize. A man who knew how to juggle a life of intrigue with a home life of normality.

She slid her left arm across his broad, bare chest and for just a moment, enjoyed the solid, warm comfort of him. And silently, she realized that as hard as his lies had been on her, how much worse it had been for him. What must it have been like for Luke, to come into their home and keep up a pretense. To never allow himself to fully relax. To always be on his guard.

Her eyes closed on a sigh as she thought about what she'd been putting him through for the last several months. Hurt, she'd attacked, wanting to be let in, wanting to know why she felt such a distance between them. And Luke must have been so torn. Wanting to take her into his confidence and not being able to.

How had he been able to do his job? How had he been able to concentrate on staying alive while worries about her were niggling at the back of his mind? Had she endangered him, however unknowingly?

"Abby?"

She turned her head and looked into his eyes. "I thought you were sleeping."

One corner of his mouth lifted. "I could hear you thinking."

Raising herself up, she braced her forearm on his chest and ran her free hand through his thick, dark hair. "I was thinking about a lot of things," she admitted.

"I'm guessing by the look in your eyes, they weren't exactly happy thoughts."

"No," she said sadly, knowing suddenly exactly what she had to say. What she had to do. "Luke, I do love you."

"I love you, too, baby." His hands swept up and down her naked back and she sighed, memorizing the feel of his fingers on her flesh.

"I know," she said, "that's what makes this so hard."

"What?" His hands stilled and his eyes narrowed.

"Luke, I'm so glad you finally told me everything. It means so much to me that you trusted me enough to be honest with me."

"Abby..." Wariness colored his voice.

She gulped in air and silently prayed for the courage she'd need to say what she had to say. "I'm still going to get a divorce."

He shot straight up, grabbing hold of her and dragging her across his lap. "What the hell are you saying?"

Lamplight threw harsh shadows over his features and his eyes glittered dangerously.

"It's the only way, Luke. The only way I can be sure you're safe. If you don't have me to worry about, you'll be able to concentrate on your job." She lifted one hand, cupped his cheek and dropped a quick kiss on his mouth. "I don't want to make you choose between your duty to your country and your marriage to me. Not anymore."

He tightened his grip on her. "Abby, I don't want a damn divorce."

"Neither do I, Luke," she said softly. "But for your sake, I'm still going to get one."

Eleven

Luke could have sworn he felt the earth literally shake beneath him. Staring into his wife's lake-blue eyes, he could hardly believe what he was hearing.

He'd thought it was settled. Thought they'd broken through the mistrust, the anger, the hurt of the past several months and found their balance. Now, when he'd finally told her everything, she wanted to leave him to protect him?

"Not a chance in hell I'm letting you go, Ab," he ground out through clenched teeth.

She wrenched herself free of his grasp, climbed off his lap and scooted off the edge of the bed. She grabbed up the nightgown she'd tossed to the floor a couple of hours ago and shimmied into it. Once she was dressed, she stabbed one finger at him and said, "We're going to get a divorce, Luke. Whether we want one or not."

He shook his head fiercely. "Do you even *hear* how stupid that sounds?"

"Stupid?" she countered. "What's stupid is sending my husband out to fight for his country and knowing that his mind isn't on his work. Worrying that he'll be thinking about me instead of protecting himself. *That* would be stupid."

"Now you're telling me how to do my job?"

"Somebody has to," she snapped.

Feeling at a decided disadvantage while naked, he jumped off the bed, grabbed his jeans and yanked them on. He didn't bother buttoning them up before stomping around the edge of the bed to stalk to her side. "Believe it or not, I'm damn good at my job. And I don't need my *wife* protecting me."

She shoved at his chest and didn't budge him an inch. "Do you think I'll be able to relax and go about with my life—lunching with the Debs, finding a new job, doing…idiotic, mundane things, all the time knowing that you're slinking through some dark alley with guns pointed at you?"

"You've got to stop watching those movies."

"So you're never in danger?"

He plowed his hands through his hair and briefly thought about snatching himself bald. And would have, if he thought it would help. "Of course there's some danger. There's danger anywhere.

Hell, Abby, you were nearly *poisoned* at a country club dance!"

"That's different."

"No, it's not," he said tightly, grabbing her upper arms and pulling her to him. "You think I would choose my job over *you?* You're wrong. I'll quit in a heartbeat if that's what it takes to keep you with me."

"I won't make you choose between me and our country, Luke."

"There are other things I can do. I don't have to be an operative."

"It's what you love," she argued.

"*You're* what I love," he said.

She dropped her forehead onto his chest and sighed heavily. "This is so hard."

His arms came around her. "Baby, it'll get better. We're going to figure all this out. We'll find out who slipped you the poison. Find Bunny's murderer. Then we'll figure out where we stand."

"We already know where we stand, Luke."

"Yeah, we do," he said, and tipped her chin up with his fingertips until his gaze met hers. "We stand *together*, Abby. Always."

At the company, Luke was like a man possessed. For two weeks, he snarled at coworkers, snapped at lab techs and growled at interns. His work was suffering because he couldn't get his mind off Abby. In that, she'd been only too right. Images of her face, her tears were with him always and he heard her voice whispering the word *divorce* over and over again in his imagination.

Every night, when he held her, when he made love to her, he promised himself he would never lose her. Then in the light of day, he was faced with her immovable decision to give him up for his own sake.

The damn woman was more stubborn than he'd given her credit for. Now that she knew who he was and what he did, she was determined to leave him—because she loved him. Now what the hell sense did *that* make?

Outside his miniscule office, the company floor was a cacophony of sound. Keyboards rattled, faxes hummed, phones rang and conversations rose and fell like waves on the ocean. But Luke wasn't a part of any of it. He'd locked himself away, not only to work, but to avoid interaction with his fellow agents. For their own good.

Everyone was walking a wide berth around him. Conversations halted when he came near and people lowered their gazes whenever he looked up from a desk that was littered with files, notes and investigative reports.

"Tom wants to see you in five."

Luke muttered a curse at the intrusion and glared up at…Katherine. His perpetual frown was replaced with a relieved grin. Good to see her up and around again. "Hey, you're looking better than the last time I saw you."

Wryly, she quipped, "Yeah, well, unconscious and bleeding's not my best look."

"You okay?"

"Yeah." She waved away his concern and strolled around the edge of his desk. "God knows we've both been through worse. Belgium springs to mind."

"True." That op had gone wrong from the start. He and Katherine had just barely managed to make the extraction point and get out to safety in time.

"You really should get yourself a better office," Katherine mused. "With your seniority, you shouldn't be working in this rat hole."

He shrugged and glanced around. "Suits me. Since I'm usually in the field, why have a big damn office sitting here empty most of the time?"

"I guess. But it's a damn mess, too." Pushing a pile of crap off the only other chair in the office, she sat down, crossed her legs and stared at him. "So, you want to tell me why Bernie's complaining about being an indentured servant?"

Luke leaned back in his chair and scrubbed both hands across his face. He'd had Bernie going over and over the tests already run on the champagne flute and its contents looking for something. Anything they might have missed. And the little lab geek was really being a pain in the ass about it.

Luke couldn't blame him. He was the best lab tech in the agency. If there had been something to find, Bernie would have found it. It was only Luke's desperation making him push the man to find the impossible.

So far, nothing. But he was determined. He had

every agent available looking for clues, trying to uncover the mystery of his mother-in-law's death.

"I need a break and Bernie's the best one to find it for me."

"Not necessarily," Katherine said and tossed the manila file folder she was holding onto his desk.

"What's this?"

"Take a look." She leaned back in her chair and smiled as she watched him. "You know how you wanted me to look into Delia Forrester? That bit with her husband's accident with the digitalis?"

"Yeah?" He flipped the folder open and quickly scanned the contents. As he read, his blood pumped and his pulse rate jumped into high gear.

"Seems dear Delia's got something of a track record when it comes to husbands. Thought you might make something of it."

Luke read the first page, then turned to the second. By the time he was finished, his eyes were flashing with determination. "This is good, Kat."

"Thought you'd like it."

"There's no evidence, though, right?"

"Not yet," Katherine said. "But there's plenty there to think about."

"Got that right," Luke agreed, tapping one finger against the file. "And I'm thinking that there's a way for us to get the proof we need."

"Just tell me what you want me to do."

Luke grinned. "I was hoping you'd say that."

* * *

"We've got something."

Abby looked up as Luke stalked across their brick patio to where she knelt in front of a flower bed, weeding. Since quitting her job and finding out the truth about her husband, she'd been too unsettled to sit still for long. And weeding gave her the satisfaction of having instant results to her work. The gardener might not appreciate her help, but being outside gave her time to think.

And heaven knew, there was plenty to think about.

She watched Luke coming toward her. Her heartbeat quickened just to see him move. She'd always felt a burst of lust whenever her husband walked into a room. But now, everything about him seemed just a little different.

Oh, he was still the man she'd always loved. But since telling her the truth about himself, it was as if Luke had decided to let her see the *real* him. His every movement radiated confidence and strength and she wondered how she had ever convinced herself that he was a man who would be satisfied sitting behind a desk.

"Abby?" He snapped his fingers in front of her face.

"What?" She blinked herself out of her daydream and grinned up at him. "Sorry. Mind wandering."

He squatted beside her and leaned in to plant a quick kiss on her mouth. Abby licked her lips as if savoring the taste of him, then took a deep breath and let it slide from her lungs on a sigh of regret. Soon, too soon, she would lose him. She would be alone, wondering what he was doing. If he was safe.

If he was missing her.

"You're doing it again," Luke said quietly, smoothing her hair back and tucking it behind her ear.

The fall sunshine was weak, but warm enough to keep the October chill at bay. A soft breeze rattled the gold and red leaves of the trees in the yard.

Abby smiled, leaned back, pulled off her gardening gloves and laid both hands on her thighs. "Okay. I'm here. Listening. Tell me."

He handed her a file folder and before she could open it, he started talking. "You already know that I've had every spare body at the company working on finding an answer to your mother's murder and the attempt on your life."

"Yes…"

"We've been looking into the backgrounds of everyone in Eastwick. Been a lot of paperwork generated on this case."

"I bet that's gone over well," she said, stroking the file folder with the tips of her fingers.

"They've been happy to help me out with this, Abby. When one of us—or our families—is attacked, everyone takes it seriously."

"What've you found?" she whispered, still a little reluctant to open that file.

"Well, the standard background checks didn't give up much. But we dug a little deeper and found something interesting." He eased down to sit on the grass opposite her. Wrapping his arms around his up-drawn knees, he gave her another quick grin and added, "In fact, found a lot of interesting stuff."

Curiosity piqued inside her, but Abby stifled it. "I don't think I want to know everyone's secrets," she said. "Mom did. She loved every little morsel of gos-sip and savored each tiny tidbit of information—" She paused and sighed. "Which is probably why she was killed, eventually. But I've recently discovered that some people have a reason for keeping secrets."

He reached out, took one of her hands and gave it a squeeze. "And some secrets," he said, "are much easier to keep when they're shared."

Linking her fingers with his, she nodded and said, "You're right. Go on. Tell me what you found."

"Most everyone here has something in their pasts that they're either not proud of, or trying to hide. But one person in particular jumped out at us."

"God," she whispered, afraid of what Luke had found out, hoping that whatever it was, it wouldn't affect someone she loved. One of her friends. "Who?"

"Delia Forrester."

Surprise jolted her a bit. Oh, Abby had never liked the woman, but she had never seemed anything other than what she appeared to be. A fortyish trophy wife of a wealthy, much-older man. Delia and Frank had only been married about a year and, though she seemed to dote on her husband, Delia hadn't really bothered to mix with the people in Eastwick. She never volunteered at the charity functions, avoided joining the club committees, and in general focused her attentions on her husband.

Sure, she was annoying and occasionally hurtful with the constant jabs and withering remarks she made a point of issuing. But what on earth could she have in her past that would so interest an investigative search of her life?

"Really?" Abby asked and kept her gaze locked on his face. "She always seems so...ordinary. Well," she corrected, "sort of *flamboyantly* ordinary, I guess."

Confused, he said, "One day, you'll have to explain to me how you can be flamboyantly ordinary."

She grinned. "Sure. But for now..."

"Right." He reached for her bottle of water, unscrewed the cap and took a long drink before speaking again. "We've looked into everyone, right down to the bartender in the Emerald Room."

"Harry?" She pulled her head back in shock and stared at him. "Please don't tell me Harry's a bad guy."

"Nope." Luke laughed. "He's just who he says he is. A cranky bartender."

"Thank God."

"Back to Delia. Remember when you told me that Frank Forrester said something once about an *accident* with his medication?"

"Yes." She recalled clearly. "He was commiserating with me after Mom's death. He even made a point of saying that Delia was going to be in charge of his medication from now on, to make sure there were no more accidents."

"Yeah, well, I'm figuring he's going to be rethinking that decision."

"Luke, tell me. What's going on?"

"First you tell me. What do you know about Delia?"

"Not much," she admitted. "She hasn't made many friends here. Seems determined *not* to. She dresses a little too flashy, her hair's a little too platinum blond and her jewelry's gaudy." Shrugging, she added, "If you didn't guess, I don't like her much."

"Glad to hear it," he said and handed her the water bottle. He waited while she took a sip, then said, "Because flashy, gaudy Delia has a background that gave a couple of very experienced agents cold chills."

"You're kidding."

"Oh, no," he said and opened the folder still lying closed on her lap. "Take a look at that."

Abby's gaze dropped to the first page of the file and her mouth dropped open when she saw Delia Forrester's mug shot. "Oh, my God."

"Yeah," Luke said wryly. "We had to go down a couple of levels to find this information. Somewhere along the line, Delia paid out some serious cash to have her file buried."

"I can't believe this."

"Well, the police photographer didn't exactly capture her best side."

"I'll say." The woman in the photograph stared out at Abby through flat, cold brown eyes. Her makeup was harsh, her hair atumble, but it was those eyes that caught and held Abby's attention. "When was this picture taken?" she asked, even as she lifted her gaze to read the information typed onto the sheet.

"About ten years ago," Luke said, and idly pulled a weed encroaching on Abby's bright gold chrysanthemums. "She was arrested for passing bad checks in New York."

"A forger?"

He nodded. "Small-time. She used to steal checks out of bill envelopes people left out on their mailboxes." He shook his head almost in admiration. "Then she'd wash the ink off, let the check dry and fill them out again for whatever she wanted."

"You can *do* that?" Astonished, Abby just stared at him.

"It's not easy, and these days, more check companies are making it even harder, with new security measures taken with the paper they use," he paused. "But yeah. Someone who knows what they're doing can make a real killing fairly easily."

"How'd she get caught?"

Luke smiled. "A cashier at an upscale department store demanded to see her ID when she wrote the check and wasn't convinced by the phony driver's license. She alerted store security, they called the local cops."

"So we know she's a thief," Abby said. "But that doesn't make her a murderer."

"I haven't gotten to the good part yet."

"There's more?"

"Plenty." Luke caught her gaze with his and held it. "Seems little Delia wasn't satisfied with petty theft. She's moved on up. Now, she's a genuine Black Widow."

A cold chill raced along Abby's spine and she shivered. "What does that mean, exactly?"

"It means that she's made a career out of marrying older, wealthy men. As far as we can tell so far, she's had five husbands—including Forrester."

"Five?"

"The kicker is, every last one of them died. Within fifteen months of marrying sweet Delia."

Twelve

"This is highly irregular," Tom Kennedy said the following day as he stood behind his desk and glared first at Luke, then at Abby, who stood by his side. "No offense, Ms. Talbot, but you don't belong here."

"Please call me Abby and, believe me, I know," she said, and would have said more, but Luke cut her off.

"This was the easiest way, Tom. She knows everything already anyway."

The huge, bald man didn't look at all happy about that little piece of news and Abby worried that Luke had compromised not only his job, but maybe his life by taking her into his confidence. What happened to spies who couldn't be spies anymore?

She glanced around the big office, idly taking in

everything at once. It was almost cavernous and as tidy as a church. Somehow it wasn't what she'd expected. But then nothing about this place was anything like her imagination had painted it. The main floor looked as though it could be any ordinary run-of-the-mill office building.

The fact that it was so nondescript, was almost a letdown.

"Yeah," Tom practically growled at him. "And we're going to be having a talk about your breach of security, real soon."

"Mr. Kennedy." Abby threaded her fingers through Luke's and held on tightly while she continued. "I'll never repeat anything my husband has told me—you have my word. And I'm happy to sign whatever paper you think is necessary."

The big man huffed out a breath, his jaw worked for a minute or two, making his substantial gray mustache twitch and then finally, he nodded abruptly. "I appreciate that, Abby. And for now, we'll just take your word at face value and leave it at that."

Luke smiled down at her and Abby felt a thread of relief unspool inside her. Even if she and Luke couldn't be together, she wanted to know that he was happy. Doing the job he loved.

She would always worry about him, but at least now, she'd have the image of his workplace in her mind and she would be able to picture him here.

"Now that that's out of the way," Luke said, keeping a tight grip on Abby's hand, "I want to talk about our plan."

"It's crazy," Katherine muttered from her chair beside the desk.

Abby looked at her briefly. Now that she knew Luke wasn't having an affair with the woman, Abby was feeling a bit more magnanimous toward her. After all, the woman had been injured in an attempt to keep Abby safe.

"It'll work," she said, meeting the woman's direct gaze.

"With you as bait," Katherine pointed out.

"I'll be right there with her," Luke said, glancing at her himself. "And so will you. Along with Baker and Hernandez. Hell, you can even bring your husband along."

"A night without the kids?" Katherine said, brightening up. "Maybe it's not so crazy after all."

Abby laughed. "You consider setting a trap for a possible killer as a good night out?"

Katherine smiled easily. "You don't know my kids."

"I do," Luke said. "She's right."

"All right now," Tom said, lifting both hands in an attempt to silence them all. "If I understand this correctly," he said, looking from one to the other of them, "you want to throw a party at your house."

"That's about the size of it," Luke agreed. "We'll invite everyone, including Delia."

"And this accomplishes…?"

"At the party," Abby put in, "we're going to trap her into a confession."

Luke nodded and took over. "There's plenty of suspicion about her former husbands' deaths, but there's no proof. If we play this right, we should be able to take her down."

"Unlikely," Tom murmured.

"I don't think so," Luke argued. "Delia's a woman on the edge. She's worried about being found out. Worried that at any moment, her past will come to light and that would be enough to get her latest husband to divorce her and run for the hills before she can get her meat hooks on his money."

"True…"

"*And,*" Abby added, "I believe she killed my mother because she had discovered something Delia wanted kept quiet. I've already put out the word that I found copies of my mother's journals and that I was going to read them before locking them up in a safety-deposit box."

"Seems risky."

Abby saw the disgusted look Tom shot at Luke and she spoke up. "Don't blame him. This was my idea. I didn't even want to tell *you,* but Luke insisted."

"Lady—" Tom started to say.

"This has nothing to do with you or your agency," Abby said, cutting him off neatly. "This is about me. And my family."

The very thought that Delia Forrester was a free woman when she might very well have killed Abby's mother was too much to stand. And from what Luke said, Bunny wasn't the woman's only victim. It was long past time that someone stopped her before other innocents died.

"She's a civilian," Tom said. "She doesn't know the dangers of—"

"I don't need your approval," Abby told him, lifting her chin and locking her gaze with the older man's. "I know what I'm doing and I insist on doing it. On my own if I have to. Doing it with your help will be a lot safer."

Luke dropped one arm around her shoulders, linking them and she was grateful for it.

"I don't like it." Tom said, then frowned when his office door flew open after a perfunctory knock. "I said no interruptions!"

"Sorry, Director," the harried-looking, middle-aged woman blurted, then shot everyone a look of apology. "But we've got trouble. Our contact in Russia is on line two and our translator is held up in traffic."

Tom stomped out from behind his desk. "Well, get someone else on it."

"There is no one else."

"Damn it, you mean to tell me there isn't one other person in this place who can speak Russian?"

"There's me," Abby offered quietly and every eye in the room turned to look at her.

"What?"

Abby shrugged. "I'd be happy to help. I do speak several languages. Always had a knack for them and—"

"Get Ms. Talbot a phone," Tom shouted, impatiently waving at Abby to hurry along with him. "Can you type, too?"

"Eighty words a minute," she said.

"That'll do," Tom said, taking her arm and practically dragging her out of the office and plunking her down into an empty cubicle.

Luke and Katherine were right behind her, watching the whole thing. Katherine looked shocked, but Luke was clearly enjoying the situation.

"Translate the information," Tom said, "and type it up exactly as you hear it. Inflections, pauses, everything. Got it?"

"Got it," Abby said, slipping the headphones on and settling behind the desk.

"Good. Get busy." Tom punched a blinking white light on the phone console.

And then Abby was too busy to think. Her fingers flew over the keyboard as the far-off Russian operative passed along information he'd gathered.

As she did the work, she smiled to herself, realizing that somehow or other, she'd just become a junior agent. She was doing something *important*. She was helping. In a very small way, she knew exactly what Luke felt when he reported to work every morning.

And she envied him.

* * *

At midnight, Abby finally gave up on trying to sleep.

She sat up, braced the pillows behind her back and stared out the French doors at the night beyond. Cold outside, the trees at the edge of the yard swayed in a wind that tore off fall leaves and tossed them like confetti.

Abby glanced at the empty bed beside her and wished Luke were there. But he was still sleeping in the guest room. With the divorce action hovering over their heads like a black cloud trying to decide whether to rain or not, Abby had told him it was best if they kept their distance.

Especially now.

Sex would only make things harder between them. How could she ever leave Luke if he was still making love to her? She closed her eyes as a wave of nausea so thick her head spun, rolled through her. Just the thought of being without Luke made her sick. How would she ever live without him in her life? How would she be able to get through the long lonely nights stretching out ahead of her through the coming years? On the other hand, how could she stay married to him, knowing his love for her might endanger him—cause him to hesitate when it might cost him his life?

Her stomach dipped again and Abby tossed the blankets back and slid off the bed. Sleep wasn't going to happen. What she needed was some hot tea. She moved quietly across the room, stopping only long enough to grab her robe from the foot of the bed. Slipping it on, she tied the green silk sash at her waist and eased her bedroom door open. No sense making enough noise to wake Luke up.

She headed downstairs, her bare feet making no sound at all on the carpeted wood steps. Shadows reached for her, but they were friendly shadows. She loved this house. Had from the moment she and Luke had first seen it. Abby had always felt safe here and the thought of leaving it broke her heart.

But she couldn't imagine living in it without Luke.

Moonlight spilled through the open windows in the dining room, and she walked through the silvery patches, with only a glance at the night sky. She walked into the kitchen and didn't bother with the light switch. She knew where everything was. Grabbing the teakettle off the stove, she took it to the sink, filled it, then set it down again on the back burner. With the gas flame shining blue in the darkness, she got down a cup and a tea bag, then sat at the kitchen table to wait.

"Isn't this handy?"

Abby jolted and spun around on her chair, staring into the dark. Her heart was still jittering in a rapid beat when Delia Forrester stepped out of the shadows. Moonlight reflected in her eyes and glinted off the edge of the knife she held in her right hand.

"Delia—"

"Please," the other woman said with a smirk. "Don't pretend to be surprised. I know you know."

"Know?" Abby stalled, looking around the kitchen, past Delia to the door into the dining room, hoping to see Luke appear like an avenging angel.

But there was nothing.

"Don't play games, I don't have the time," Delia snapped and stepped up close, grabbing Abby with one hand and holding the knife in front of her face with the other. "I want the copies of your mother's journals."

Damn. Abby had expected Delia to make a move for the diaries at the party they'd planned. For some reason, she had never thought the woman would break into the house and try for them early. Stupid.

"*Now,* Abby," Delia warned.

"Fine. Fine. They're in the, uh…" She remembered finally where she and Luke had told everyone they'd stashed the nonexistent copies of the journals. "Living room."

"Great. Let's go." Delia yanked her out of the chair and Abby had a moment to wonder if the woman was really that strong, or did crazy people just get a burst of muscle when they needed it most?

Prodding her across the floor, Delia kept the knife close to Abby's side as they left the kitchen. Halfway across the dining room, an earsplitting whistle sounded—the teakettle on the stove had reached the boiling point.

Delia hesitated, then gave Abby a push. "Never mind. Hurry up. Get the journals and I'm out of here."

Fear shaking inside her, Abby stepped into the living room and walked toward the farthest book-case. Her gaze swept the room, calculating escape plans. Looking for something to use as a weapon. Bottles of liquor? Too far away. Lamp? Too heavy to grab and throw in time. Damn it. *Luke! Wake up!*

She had to do something, Abby thought wildly, as the very real fear of dying grabbed at her and wouldn't let go.

"Drop the knife, Delia." Luke turned on the lights at the same time as he spoke and there was a brief moment of sheer blindness, going from dark to light so quickly.

But Delia recovered far faster than Abby did. She grabbed hold of Abby, spun her around to face Luke and held the knife close to her captive's rib cage. "Back off now, or I'll kill her."

"No you won't."

God, he looked good. And fierce. Like an avenging angel. His dark eyes were narrowed and full of fury. She'd wished for him and here he was. Like her own personal cavalry.

Delia laughed and the sound was like nails on a chalkboard. Abby winced, but Luke never flinched. Barefoot, in jeans, his features grim, he braced himself and held his pistol in both hands, its barrel pointed at Delia.

"I can drop you right here," he promised.

"Not before I cut her, you can't."

"I've got a shot," someone else said and Delia darted a look at the far corner, as Katherine Shaker stepped out from behind a leather couch where she'd been hidden.

"Me, too." Another man's voice, this time coming from behind the bar.

"Damn it!" Delia's voice hitched as she muttered the curse and her grip on Abby tightened even further. "I swear to God I'll kill her. I've done it before. One more dead bitch won't bother me."

"Touch her and you're dead."

"So predictable," Delia hissed. "Men are so damn easy. You want to be her white knight? Then back off before you get her killed."

Abby's gaze remained locked on Luke and she didn't look away when he idly waved off the agent behind the wet bar.

"It was all so easy," Delia muttered, more talking to herself than anything else. "All those men, so easy to make them fall in love with me. Even easier to kill them. Disgusting, slobbering old farts. Did they really think I *wanted* them? Men. As a gender, you're all pretty useless," she pointed out to Luke. "It took a *woman* to figure it all out."

"My mother?" Abby whispered and for her trouble, felt the edge of the knife press through the sheer fabric of her robe and into her side. She yelped as a trickle of blood rolled down her skin.

"Keep still," Delia said with a sneer. "Don't want me to get nervous, do you?"

"I'm okay," Abby shouted to Luke and winced as the knife bit into her again.

"Your mother just kept sticking her nose into my business," Delia muttered as if she still couldn't believe it had all gone so wrong so fast. "You're just like her. Questions. Always questions. The bitch should have understood! She should have been on *my* side. Woman to woman. But no. She didn't see it that way. So she had to go."

"You killed my mother."

"Not like I wanted to," Delia argued. "She didn't give me a choice. It was her own damn fault. Nosy bitch was asking for it."

Abby saw red. Actual red. The edges of her vision clouded and swam with the fury nearly choking her. Before she could think about it, before she could worry about the repercussions, she spun out of Delia's hold, turned and slammed her closed fist into the other woman's jaw.

Delia staggered back as if she'd been hit by a truck and before she could recover, Luke was there, knocking the knife out of her hand and pushing the older woman to the floor. In a couple of seconds, he had her facedown on the carpet, wearing a shiny pair of handcuffs and screaming about revenge and the stupidity of men in general.

While the other agent dragged Delia to the car waiting outside, Katherine sprinted to the kitchen to turn off the still-shrieking teakettle.

Luke gathered Abby in his arms and held on tight.

"Ow," Abby complained as his grip came down on the slice in her side. Instantly, he released her.

"God, you idiot, she could have killed you," he

murmured, pushing her robe aside and lifting her night-gown to get a look at the cut. "Going to need stitches."

"Great," Abby said shakily, "I hate needles."

Then she swayed a little unsteadily and Luke grabbed her again, face tucked into the curve of her neck.

"She killed Mom," Abby said, squirming in as close as she could get to her husband's broad, bare chest. "And she wasn't sorry. She just made me so mad, I—"

"It's all over now, baby. It's over." He ran one hand over her hair and the other up and down her spine, as if reassuring himself of her safety.

"How'd you know she was here?" Abby asked, her voice muffled against him.

"I followed you when you went downstairs. Katherine and Hank were positioned in here just in case Delia made a preemptive strike for the journals."

"Good call," she managed to say.

"Thanks."

In the background, the teakettle's whistle abruptly ended and Abby knew that it was all over. God, she couldn't believe it. She was safe. Luke was safe. And her mother's killer was going to be behind bars for a long, long time.

"Luke?" Katherine called from the doorway and he looked up. "We're taking the nutball into the company for interrogation. You want to be there?"

"In an hour or two. First I'm taking Abby to the hospital. The bitch cut her."

Katherine scowled and glanced at Abby. "You gonna be okay?"

"Yes. Thanks."

The other woman smiled, lifted one hand and walked out the front door, closing it behind her.

"It's over."

"Not yet," Luke said and stepped back from her only far enough that he could cup her face in his hands. Looking into her eyes, he said tightly, "I know you've got some big ideas about leaving me for my own good, but I'm not letting you go, Abby."

"Luke…"

"I'm through being a spy," he said, staring into her eyes, willing her to believe him. "There are lots of jobs I can do for the company without being a field agent. From now on, I'm only playing secret agent with you. In our bedroom."

Abby looked up at him through teary eyes and oh God, she really wanted to let him make that sacrifice. She didn't want to go through life without him. But… "You'll regret that decision. You know you will. Luke, I don't want you to resent me someday for forcing you to give up the job you love."

"You're not forcing me to do anything. I made my choice Abby. It's you."

"I wish it was that easy."

"It *is*," he said softly, a gentle smile curving his amazing mouth. "It's only hard if you fight me on it. And I warn you, you'll lose."

His eyes were so warm and dark and full of love,

it stole her breath. And Abby so wanted to let him do this. Yet still, she hesitated.

He bent down, pressed his lips to hers for a long second or two, then straightened up and said, "The only thing I would ever regret is losing *you*. Nothing means anything to me without you in my life, Abby. Don't you get that?"

Everything she needed to know was in his eyes. His voice. His touch.

"I do," she said, smiling now, even as the tears rolled down her face. "I love you so much, Luke. And I don't want to lose you, either."

He exhaled and gave her a grin that made her toes tingle. "Never gonna happen, babe."

She reached up to hug him and yelped as the pain in her side screamed at her.

"Right," Luke said, scooping her up into his arms. "First things first. Stitches. Then interrogating the bitch from hell."

"Can I watch?" she asked, cuddling in close to her own personal Secret Agent Man.

"Wouldn't have it any other way," Luke told her, and headed for the front door.

They had the planned party anyway a few nights later.

With smooth jazz sliding from the stereo, and all of her friends gathered in her home, Abby smiled and enjoyed the sensation of having everything right with her world. Her gaze slanted over the couples laughing and talking and she smiled at all of them.

Jack and Lily had brought baby Grace with them—they couldn't bear to be apart from her just yet. Emma and Garret were standing close to them and the look in Emma's eyes told Abby that babies were definitely on her good friend's mind. Felicity and Reid were dancing, oblivious to everyone else and Mary and Kane were standing in a corner arguing about something—and clearly enjoying the spirited debate. Vanessa and Tristan were talking to Katherine Shaker and her husband and Abby grinned. Katherine had demanded her invitation to the party be upheld. She had really wanted a night out.

And then there was Luke, smiling at her from across the room. Her heart jumped in her chest and she dropped one hand to her abdomen. God, just a month ago, she never would have believed she could be this happy. She took a sip of her tonic water and lime and held out one hand to Luke when he came toward her.

"Thanks for coming, everybody," Luke said just loudly enough to get everyone's attention.

Emma grinned. "How could we resist? Not only a party, but the answers to what's been going on in Eastwick."

Luke dropped one arm around Abby's shoulders and gave her a squeeze. "Right. Well, you all know Delia Forrester's been arrested."

"Still can't believe she actually killed Bunny," Mary murmured.

"Believe it. There's no clear evidence to prove that she also killed all of her previous husbands, but there's enough suspicion that I don't believe she's going to be getting out of jail any time soon."

"But why?" Felicity asked. "Why Bunny?"

Abby spoke up. "Apparently, Mom was there when Frank had some chest pains and she noticed that until Delia spotted Mom watching, she was moving really slow in getting help. But Mom didn't realize that she'd actually thwarted a murder attempt."

"Until much later," Luke added.

"Right," Abby said. "You know that Mom wrote down *everything* in her journals. Well, I guess she started keeping an eye on Delia after that. Making notes, tracking little things. Enough to make Delia worry about her. Eventually, Delia decided to kill Mom the way she had planned to kill Frank. By replacing Mom's digitalis with placebos." She looked over at Mary. "The day Mom died, Delia saw Mary leave Mom's house after an argument."

Mary dipped her head, but Kane gave her a supportive hug that had her smiling a moment later.

"When Mary left Bunny," Luke said, taking up the story, "Delia slipped inside and forced Bunny at gunpoint to hand over her journals. The stress and fear sent Bunny into cardiac arrest. She tried to take one of her pills, but dropped it as she died. Delia says she took the pills with her when she left, but apparently, she missed the one Bunny dropped when the housekeeper's approach sent her running."

"Good God," Garrett muttered.

"Poor Bunny," Felicity said.

"A while later," Luke started talking again, "Delia phoned Kane, disguised her voice and implicated Mary in Bunny's death."

"What about all of the other blackmail attempts after Bunny died?" Vanessa asked.

"It seems that killing Bunny was about self-preservation," Luke said, hugging Abby again. "But the other blackmail attempts were just about greed. And spite. We found all of Bunny's journals hidden away in Delia's house."

"They're still around?" Mary whispered.

"Don't worry," Abby said, smiling. "I burned them myself last night."

"Good," Jack said. "I think Eastwick's had enough of the scandalous."

"Amen to that," Reid said.

"Well, I don't know," Abby told them all, snaking one arm around her husband's waist. "I have had an anonymous offer to continue Mom's column. It seems someone out there thinks there are still plenty of scandals to write about."

"Oh, no," Emma said, laughing. "You're kidding."

Everyone laughed and talked at once and in the hubbub, Luke leaned down to whisper into his wife's ear. "So, are you going to tell them all about your new job?"

"I think that can wait. After all, to all of them, it'll only look like I'm going to work at your company with you. No one will ever know that I'm a translator for spies." She could hardly believe it herself. But her shiny new ID badge was real enough.

He wiggled his eyebrows and winked at her. "Now we can ride to work together."

"Except for next week," she reminded him. "When you'll be in Hong Kong."

Luke's smile faded and he looked a little worried. "Just this one more mission, baby. I swear."

Abby ignored her friends and concentrated solely on the man she loved. "Don't worry. I know just how good you are at your job. And now that I'm an assistant spy, I'll be able to keep closer tabs on you."

"I call that a win," Luke said, dropping a kiss on her forehead. "So. You feeling okay? You need to sit down or something?"

Abby laughed in delight. She felt as though she'd been grinning like an idiot ever since Luke had taken her to the hospital to be stitched up and the doctors had discovered she was *pregnant*. "Luke, I came through a car accident and a near stabbing by a psycho. I'm fine. *We're* fine."

"Damn right you are." His mouth curved again. "Do you want to make the announcement, or do you want me to do it?"

"Let's do it together," she said, threading her fingers in his.

"Always, baby," he said. "Always."

Then, he raised his voice, lifted his glass and called out, "Everybody, we'd like to make a toast."

"To what?" Someone asked.

Abby lifted her glass, too, looked at Luke with love shining in her eyes, then with him, she faced their friends and they both said, "To our baby."

Cheers roared and soon they were surrounded by all of the people who were most important to them. And when the last congratulations had been said, Abby lifted her glass again, looked at every one of her friends in turn and knew she'd never been happier. Each of them had been through so much in the last year. And they'd all come out the other side, stronger. Happier.

The circle of her friends gathered around her and she said softly, "To the Debs. Friends forever."

* * * * *

RUN, ALLY! Don't be fooled by him. He's evil. Don't let him touch you!

But as the forbidding figure came through the mists toward her, Ally knew she couldn't run. His features burned with dark malevolence, and his physical domination of everything around him seemed to hold her like a net.

She'd heard the tales. She knew all about the Wolverton legend and the ghost that haunted The Willows, an elegant old mansion lost by Micha Wolverton nearly a hundred years ago. According to folklore, the estate was stolen from the Wolvertons, and Micha was killed, trying to reclaim it. His dying vow was to be reunited with the spirit of his beloved wife, who'd taken her life for reasons no one would speak of, except in whispers. But Ally had never put much stock in the fantasy. She didn't believe in ghosts.

Until now—

She still didn't understand what was happening. The figure had materialized out of the mist that lay thick on the damp cemetery soil. A cool breeze and silvery moonlight had played against the ancient stone of the crypts surrounding her, until they joined the mist, causing his body to thicken and solidify right before her eyes. That was when she realized she'd seen this man before. Or thought she had, at least.

His face was familiar…so familiar, yet she couldn't put it together. Not with him looming so near. She stepped back as he approached.

"Don't be afraid," he said. His voice wasn't what she expected. It didn't sound as if it were coming from beyond the grave. It was deep and sensual. Commanding.

"Who are you?" she managed.

"You should know. You summoned me."

"No, I didn't." She had no idea what he was talking about. Two minutes ago, she'd been crouching behind a moss-covered crypt, spying on the mansion that had once been The Willows, but was now Club Casablanca. And then this—

If he was Micah, he might be angry that she was trespassing on his property. "I'll go," she said. "I won't come back. I promise."

"You're not going anywhere."

Words snagged in her throat. "Wh-why not? What do you want?"

"If I wanted something, Ally, I'd take it. This is about need."

His words resonated as he moved within inches of her. She tried to back away, but her feet were useless. "And you need something from me?"

"Good guess." His tone burned with irony. "I need lips, soft and surrendered, a body limp with desire."

"My lips, my bod—?"

"Only yours."

"Why? Why me?" This couldn't be Micha. He didn't want any woman but Rose. He'd died trying to get back to her.

"Because you want that, too," he said.

Wanted what? A ghost of her own? She'd always found the legend impossibly romantic, but how could he have known that? How could he know anything about her? Besides, she'd sworn off inappropriate men, and what could be more inappropriate than a ghost? She shook her head again, still not willing to admit the truth. But her heart wouldn't play along. It clattered inside her chest. The mere thought of his kiss, his touch, terrified her. This wildness, it was fear, wasn't it?

When his fingertips touched her cheek, she flinched, expecting his flesh to be cold, lifeless. It was anything but that. His skin was smooth and hot, gentle, yet demanding. And while his dark brown eyes were filled with mystery and wonder, there was a sensitivity about them that threatened to disarm her if she looked too deeply.

"These lips are mine," he said, as if stating a universal fact that she was helpless to avoid. In truth, it was just that. She couldn't stop him.

And she didn't want to.

* * * * *

Find out how the story unfolds in...
DECADENT
by
New York Times *bestselling author*
Suzanne Forster.
On sale November 2006.

Harlequin Blaze—Your ultimate destination
for red-hot reads.
With six titles every month, you'll never guess
what you'll discover under the covers...

REQUEST YOUR FREE BOOKS!

2 FREE NOVELS PLUS 2 FREE GIFTS!

Passionate, Powerful, Provocative!

nocturne™

USA TODAY bestselling author

MAUREEN CHILD

ETERNALLY

He was a guardian. An immortal fighter of evil,
out to destroy a demon, and she was his next
target. He knew joining with her would make
him strong enough to defeat any demon.
But the cost might be losing the woman
who was his true salvation.

On sale November, wherever books are sold.

COMING NEXT MONTH